**Hope ...**

*Christmas ...*

It's a time of miracles and magic—and as Hope Children's Hospital prepares to celebrate its first Christmas in the historic city of Cambridge, England, the staff will do everything they can to make their little patients' wishes come true.

Billionaire CEO Theo Hawkwood leads a world-renowned handpicked medical team who strive to give the best treatment to their precious charges, and hope to all who come through the doors. This Christmas, they'll discover that miracles can be found in the most unexpected of places— and love will prove the greatest gift of all!

*Their Newborn Baby Gift*
by Alison Roberts

*One Night, One Unexpected Miracle*
by Caroline Anderson

*The Army Doc's Christmas Angel*
by Annie O'Neil

*The Billionaire's Christmas Wish*
by Tina Beckett

All available now!

Dear Reader,

When I was asked to take part in this continuity, I was excited to see that it incorporated two of my favorite elements: a children's hospital and Christmas. My answer, of course, was an enthusiastic yes!

My two main characters, however, didn't share my excitement for Christmas. My job was to somehow coax them to change their minds. And, boy, that wasn't easy. Theo Hawkwood and Madison Archer were determined that they were fine just the way they were.

Thank you for joining Theo and Maddy as they struggle to let go of the past. And hopefully this special couple will discover a little magic waiting for them at the end of their journey. I hope you enjoy reading their story as much as I loved writing it.

Love,

*Tina Beckett*

# THE BILLIONAIRE'S
# CHRISTMAS WISH

———

## TINA BECKETT

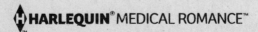
HARLEQUIN® MEDICAL ROMANCE™

Special thanks and acknowledgment are given
to Tina Beckett for her contribution to the
Hope Children's Hospital series.

Recycling programs
for this product may
not exist in your area.

ISBN-13: 978-1-335-66389-4

The Billionaire's Christmas Wish

First North American Publication 2018

Copyright © 2018 by Harlequin Books S.A.

Printed in U.S.A.

www.Harlequin.com

To my family.
You bring me joy each and every day.

**Praise for
Tina Beckett**

"This is a truly passionate and moving story
that brings two beautiful people together....
Ms. Beckett has brought out the love and emotion
that will surely have you smiling and sighing."
—*Goodreads* on *Rafael's One Night Bombshell*

# CHAPTER ONE

"THEO—IVY IS asking for you."

Theo Hawkwood's heart dropped into the acidic pool in his stomach as the nurse's voice came through his cellphone.

"Is she okay?"

Of course she wasn't. His daughter hadn't been "okay" for months. Which was why she'd been moved to a room a short distance from his office.

"There's no change. I think she just wants to see you."

A familiar nagging ache went through his chest, filling the space his heart had just vacated. His wife's sudden death four and a half years ago had left him with a hole in his life and an infant daughter to raise. And now Ivy was sick. Very sick. And no one could tell him why. If he lost her too...

*You won't. You have one of the best diagnosticians in the world on the case.*

Except even she was stumped.

"I'm on my way. Can you find Dr. Archer for me?"

"She's already there. She's the one who asked me to call you."

Shoving his phone into the pocket of his jeans, he pushed away from the desk and the pile of requisitions he'd been studying. Once on his feet, he dragged a hand through his hair. It had been months. And still no definitive diagnosis. They knew what it wasn't but not what it was that was making Ivy's arms and legs grow weaker by the day. As unfair as it was, he'd been pinning all his hopes on Madison Archer, only to have them dashed time and time again.

Striding across the bridge that joined his section of the hospital with the area that housed the family suites, he tried to avoid looking at the festive ribbons and lights that twinkled with the joy of the season. Joy? He just wasn't feeling it. As much as he tried to put on a cheerful face for the sake of his daughter, the storms raging inside him were anything but cheerful. How long before Ivy noticed?

Maybe she already had.

He took his gaze from the decorations and fixed them straight ahead until he came to Ivy's room. He didn't bother knocking, just pushed quietly through the door then stopped in his tracks. Madison was seated on the side of his daughter's bed, their heads close together, and they were…laughing.

Had he ever actually heard Madison laugh?

He didn't think so. She was professional to a fault. He'd even overheard the word "Scrooge" attributed to her after she'd refused to give an opinion on the lights on the banister leading to the family suites. A quick glance from him had silenced the comment in mid-sentence.

And now? The deep copper highlights of the diagnostician's hair cascaded in waves that covered the side of her face so he couldn't see her, but she was writing something in a small notebook. She giggled again. "Are you sure?"

"Yes," his daughter replied.

Something in his gut gave a painful jerk. "What's going on in here?"

The second the gruff question came out of his mouth the laughter came to an abrupt halt, and Madison slammed the notebook shut.

He wished he could take the words back. Wished he could take a whole lot of things back, but he couldn't.

Madison's face came into view as she shook her hair back to peer up at him, her indrawn brows causing tiny puckers to form between them.

Hell, he needed to get a grip. The nurse's message a few moments earlier had made him think something was wrong, and he'd buzzed in here like some kind of hornet, looking for something or someone to strike.

Only there was no one. Only some mystery illness that refused to poke its head out so it could be seen for what it was.

A stealer of life. A stealer of joy.

For Theo, the feeling of helplessness was the worst sensation in the world. Worse than the loss of his wife to a drunk driver over four years ago. At least that had been something concrete that he could understand. He'd known exactly where to place the blame that time. But this time there was nothing.

"Are you okay?" Madison's smile had morphed into professional concern, her fingers balancing her pen over the notebook. Scrooge? Hell, he was the Scrooge, not her.

"I'm sorry. You called me down here, and I

thought…" His voice trailed away and a lump formed in his throat when Ivy didn't immediately jump off her bed and squeeze his legs in a tight hug, like she used to.

She couldn't. Ivy couldn't even walk now.

The diagnostician tucked the pen and book into the front pocket of her long gray tunic and then got up and stood in front of him. Those long legs of hers brought her almost to eye level. She still had to tilt her head a bit, but she didn't have to crane her neck like Hope used to do.

He swallowed and threw another log onto the fire of guilt.

"Hey." Her fingers landed on his arm with a quick squeeze that sent something skittering up his spine to his brain—a flash of something he had no intention of analyzing. "Don't you quit on me."

She didn't have to translate the meaning for him, and Theo was smart enough to nod at her subtle warning not to scare his daughter unnecessarily.

But how about him? He was scared out of his mind right now.

"No quitting involved." His voice sounded a lot more sure than he felt. Even so, he softened his tone for the next part. "So I'll ask again. What's going on?"

"We were just making some plans for... Christmas."

He blinked. There had been an awkward pause before she'd added that last word. And the way she'd blurted it out—like she couldn't wait to fling it off her tongue—made him wonder.

Was it because she wasn't sure Ivy was even going to be around to celebrate the event, which was a short two weeks away? That thought sent icy perspiration prickling across his upper lip. "Plans for?"

Ivy, who had been silent for the exchange, said, "For Sanna Claus. And your presents."

Her mispronunciation of good old Saint Nick's name made him smile, relief making his shoulders slump. It had become a running joke between them, with him correcting her and Ivy persisting in leaving out the "t" sound with a nose crinkled in amusement.

He glanced at his daughter and then at Madison. "The only present I need is for you to get better, sweetheart."

He put a wealth of meaning into those words and aimed them at the diagnostician.

Uncertainty shimmered in the green depths

of the other doctor's eyes and his relief fled in an instant. Theo knew how she felt, though. Before he'd founded the hospital—back when he'd been a practicing surgeon—there'd been a few cases where he'd been unable to promise the family a good outcome. He'd still done his damnedest for those patients despite seemingly impossible odds. Was Madison feeling that same pressure? Worse, did she think Ivy's case was hopeless?

Unable to face what that might mean, he turned his attention to Ivy. "Have you been out of bed yet today?"

"Yes. Madison helped me." Ivy took the rag doll she carried everywhere with her and struggled to lift it to her chest in a hug. "I had to leave Gerty on the bed. She was too heavy today."

The ache in his chest grew. Hope had made that doll for their daughter a few months before she'd given birth to Ivy.

"Wheelchair? Or walking?" He kept his eyes on his daughter, even though the question was directed at Madison.

The other doctor went over and laid a hand on Ivy's head. "I'm going to have a chat with your dad outside, okay? You keep thinking about that list."

Right on cue, Ivy yawned. "I will."

Madison led the way through the door. Once it swung shut, she said, "She'll be asleep in five minutes."

Was she avoiding answering his question? "Wheelchair or walking?"

"She hasn't walked in a week, Theo. You know that."

"Yes. But I'd hoped…" His eyes shut for several long seconds. "Tell me again what we've ruled out."

"Did you get the list I emailed you? Your staff had already ruled out most of the obvious conditions before I arrived." She tucked a lock of hair behind her ear, fingers worrying the ends for a second or two before continuing. "There is no brain tumor. No lesions that suggest something is going on with the synaptic connections. And the results of the muscle biopsy I ordered came back yesterday. There's no sign of limb-girdle muscular dystrophy."

She must have seen something in his face because she hurried to add, "That's a good thing."

"Then why are her arms and legs getting progressively weaker?" As relieved as he should be that there was no sign of the deadly condition, his inability to help his daughter made his voice rough-edged yet again.

"I don't know." She pulled in a deep breath and blew it back out. "But I'm still going down a list of possibilities. I just don't want to rush through them and overlook something and then have to double back. Wasted time can't be recaptured."

No, it couldn't. What was gone was gone.

He did his best to ignore those last words and tried to focus on the positive: she hadn't exhausted everything. Not yet, at least.

"Multiple sclerosis?" Although MS normally affected adults, he'd researched everything he could think of and had found cases where children were diagnosed with it.

"Again, there's no sign of brain lesions. I went over the MRI scans with a fine-toothed comb. I saw no anomalies at all."

"Damn."

A tug at his sleeve brought his eyes back to hers. "I told you I'd tell you when to worry. We're not there yet."

"Yes, we are. I can see it in your face."

"It's not that I'm worried. I'm just frustrated I don't have an answer for you. I'm exploring every avenue I can think of." Her fingers tightened.

"I know you are, Madison. I'm treating you like Ivy is your only patient, and I know that's not true."

"I'm here for her and for patients just like her. She has a great team of specialists fighting on her behalf, and I'm grateful to be included in that. Ivy is a big part of Hope Children's Hospital."

Named after his late wife, who'd waited patiently in the wings for him to break ground on his dream, even putting her own career on hold to look after Ivy while he'd worked day and night. She'd died before seeing the fruits of their labor or being able to practice medicine again. And he damned himself every single day for not spending more time with her and Ivy while his wife had still been here.

*"Wasted time can't be recaptured."*

Truer words had never been spoken.

He leaned a shoulder against the wall and turned to fully face her. Her fingers let go of his sleeve in the process.

"Anything I can do to help?" he asked.

"Just throw out any ideas that might help—even if they seem farfetched. I sent a panel off looking for some markers of Lyme disease or any of the co-infections that might be related to it. I should have something back in a few days."

"Lyme. Is that even a possibility? I keep going back to it being a brain issue."

Madison's brow puckered the way it had back in Ivy's room. She was either thinking or irritated. Maybe she thought he was challenging her readings of the MRI scans. He wasn't. He just couldn't get past the possibility that something in Ivy's head was misfiring or inhibiting signals. The condition mimicked one of the muscular dystrophies. But the biopsies said it wasn't. So if it wasn't in the muscles themselves...

"I thought for sure it was too. But there's nothing there, Theo."

Every time she used his name, something coiled inside him. Lots of people called him by his given name rather than his professional title, but that husky American accent, devoid of the crisp consonants that peppered the speech of those in Britain, warmed parts of him that had been frozen in time and space.

She provided hope. A fresh perspective. She was unconventional, could think outside the box. Her files listed one of her weaknesses as being her hard-nosed approach. She had difficulty being a team player, and she wasn't afraid to question findings or demand a test be run again if it wasn't done to her satisfaction. He didn't see that as a weakness. In this case he viewed her reputation as a strength, which was why he hadn't insisted she attend the staff meetings related to Ivy's care.

She'd made a few enemies back home—and even here in Cambridge. But she'd also made friends. And one of those friends appeared to be his daughter.

"Where do you look next? She's had no headaches. No symptoms other than the growing weakness in her limbs. And wondering whether that weakness is going to progress to her breathing or autonomic nervous system is making me—"

"Crazy? I know. It's making us all a little crazy. That kid has a lot of people wrapped around her little finger."

"Yes, she does." He smiled. "Including her father."

Her fingers toyed with the edge of his sleeve again, not quite touching him, as if she wanted to give comfort but was afraid of skin-to-skin contact. "We're going to figure this out."

Right now he was *glad* she wasn't touching him. Because the warm flow of her voice was doing what her hand wasn't. It was permeating his pores and meandering through his bloodstream, where it affected his breathing, his heart rate and his thoughts—taking them into dangerous territory. Territory that only his late wife had occupied. He couldn't afford to let Madison trespass there. If he did, it could spell disaster for both him and his daughter.

"I'm sure you will." In a deliberate move, he tugged his sleeve from her grasp. "I'm counting on it. And so is Ivy."

Then he was walking away, before he could ask exactly what she and Ivy had been planning for Christmas, or ask if Madison was including herself in those plans.

Once back in the tiny office she'd been given while Dr. Camargo's office was being renovated, Madison fingered the notebook in her pocket. She was glad that Theo hadn't asked her to hand it over to him. He'd seemed pretty upset to find the two of them in there laughing, but it hadn't been easy to pretend when her heart was aching over the little girl's revelation. Because the first thing on Ivy's wish list was for her father to like Christmas.

Her eyes had burned. It seemed that she wasn't the only one with an aversion to the season. And the last thing she could promise anyone was that she'd help them learn to like a holiday she detested. Maybe she should put that on her Christmas list too.

Except Madison had no interest in changing her ways at this late date. She did what she could to get through the last month of the year, closed her eyes as she passed the festive trees and lights, and then breathed a sigh of relief once the calendar rolled over into a new year.

Fingering the thick file folder on her desk, she flipped it open to the first page, where Ivy's vital statistics were listed in bold clinical letters. The child was far wiser than her five years. And she saw things Theo probably didn't even know she was aware of. Or maybe his daughter had already shared her longing with him. Madison didn't think so, though.

She knew he was widowed, from the hospital grapevine. And his ring finger no longer held a wedding ring, so he'd gotten over the loss. Or had he? Some people never really got over that kind of life change.

Another thing Madison could relate to. Although her loss had nothing to do with a husband, or even a boyfriend.

Shaking herself free of her funk, she pulled the notebook from her pocket and dropped it onto her desk. She'd have to figure out a way to get a few of the things on Ivy's list without making her dad suspicious. Or angry. He had to know how fortunate he was to have a daughter who was worried as much about him as he worried about her. She was small and so very ill, and yet her determination to do all she could to get better—for her dad's sake—was one of the most touching things Madison had seen in a long time.

She flipped the first page open and perused the list, forcing her glance to leap over that first item. The rest of the things ranged from sweet to hilarious.

*A new stethoscope—in purple, if Santa has one, because that is Ivy's favorite color.*

*A book about horses so he'll fall in love with them like she has.*

*An adult coloring book. One of Ivy's nurses talked about how every grown-up should have one.*

Somehow, Madison couldn't picture those big hands clutching a crayon—although he was very much a paint-by-numbers type of person. No coloring outside the lines for him.

*Macaroni and cheese. Evidently Theo's favorite food. Santa must carry casseroles around in his toy sack.*
*A puppy. Ha! Wouldn't Theo love coming home to find a puppy under the tree.*

That was all they had so far on the list. Except for that very first thing. Her eyes tracked up to it against their will.

*Make Daddy love Christmas.*

God, even the real Santa would have a tough time granting that wish. The rest was doable. Well, maybe not the puppy. But everything else could be gotten for a relatively inexpensive price, wrapped and listed as being from Santa.

Why did she even care? She wasn't here to buy anyone gifts. Or to make a little girl happy.

She was here to help solve difficult diagnoses. That was it. And to fulfill a lifelong dream of visiting the UK. She should be on cloud nine. Instead, she felt itchy and slightly uncomfortable, like wearing a new wool sweater without anything else beneath it.

*You need to get out and see more of England. Staying around this hospital day in and day out isn't healthy.*

But there was something about Ivy...

She'd found herself spending more and more time with the little girl, almost succeeding in convincing herself it was to help figure out the child's condition. Except she knew it was a lie. She was here for Ivy, even if being around her dad made her squirm in discomfort.

She wasn't exactly sure why that was, but she'd better figure it out before she did something stupid. Really stupid. Like wish Ivy were hers, maybe?

She stood in a rush and clasped her hands behind her back, lifting them away from her body while bending forward at the waist, hoping the resultant stretch would help clear her head of its current thoughts. Higher and harder she stretched, vaguely aware of her door opening with a couple of light taps.

"Dr. Archer?"

Madison froze in place. Oh, Lordy. But at

least the voice was female and not the man who'd jerked away from her a couple of hours earlier. How humiliating had that been? She'd just been trying to help.

Letting her arms drop back to her sides, she stood and saw Naomi Collins, one of the physical therapists at the hospital. Her romance with pediatric surgeon Finn Morgan was the stuff dreams were made of.

"Hi. Sorry about that. I had a kink in my neck and was trying to work it out." More like a kink in her head, but it was pretty much the same thing.

Naomi chuckled. "It's fine. You should see the things I do when I'm alone." Another laugh. "Forget I said that. I didn't mean that quite the way it sounded."

"I didn't think it sounded odd at all." She smiled to reassure her. After all, if Naomi could have gotten a good look at what was rattling around in her head, she might be a little more than shocked. "Can I help you with something?"

"I just wanted to talk with you about Ivy. What you wanted me to work on with her tomorrow."

With her clear complexion and deep gorgeous skin tones, Naomi was beautiful. And she was a huge hit with all her young charges, including Ivy.

"I'm not her only doctor, you know."

Naomi entered the office and closed the door behind her. "Maybe not, but right now everyone—if they're smart—is deferring to you and hoping you'll solve whatever is going on with her."

"And if I can't?" The words that she hadn't dared say aloud in the hallway with Theo came tumbling out before she could stop them. She dropped into one of the metal chairs that flanked her desk.

The physical therapist came over and sat in the other one. "It's a bit of pressure, yes?"

"Yes. And I want to figure it out. But I'm at a dead end at the moment." She didn't know why she was suddenly voicing her fears, but there was something in the other woman's eyes that said she'd known fear—intimately—and had come out on the other side.

"Sometimes we just have to give ourselves a bit of space to regroup. And that's when it normally comes to us. That realization that's been in front of us all along."

Were they still talking about Ivy? Or about something else?

"I hope you're right."

"I am. You'll see." Naomi leaned forward and captured her hands. "Just give yourself permission to take a step or two back and look at the problem with a wide-angle lens."

Something about those words caught at an area of her brain, which set to work in the background. "Thank you. I think I needed to hear that." She squeezed the other woman's fingers before letting go. Gently. Not the way Theo had done in the hallway. "How are things with you and Finn, if I may ask?"

Naomi's smile caused her nose to crinkle in a way that was both adorable and mischievous. "You can. And it's great. Better than I have a right to expect."

"It's exactly what you *should* expect. And what you deserve." From what Madison had heard, Naomi had had a hard time of it, losing loved ones in a terrible conflict in her home country. But she'd overcome it and had learned to live her life in the present.

Maybe Naomi should write a how-to book on how to do that. Madison would be one of her first customers if that ever happened.

"Thank you. Finn's a good man." Naomi sucked down a deep breath and squared her shoulders. "Now, about Ivy…"

Madison went over what she would like to

see happen with Ivy's therapy tomorrow. Although she couldn't walk or even hold herself up on the parallel bars they used to help people learn to walk again, they could still try to utilize what muscle strength she did have to its best advantage. Having her kick a large exercise ball and do some resistance bands to hopefully keep things from atrophying any faster than they already were was the biggest goal at the moment.

"I agree. That's the perfect thing for her. I did a little work with the bands today, in fact. Right now the hope is to slow that downward spiral as much as possible, to buy ourselves time to find whatever's going on."

"Yes, and thank you. Do you want me to check with Theo to make sure he agrees?"

Naomi shook her head. "He'll agree. He's desperate to find anything that will work. As are we all. We all want her to beat whatever this is."

With that she stood to her feet. "I think I'll check in on her on my way out."

"Thank you. And thanks for the pep talk."

The physical therapist fixed her with a look. "It wasn't a pep talk. It was the truth."

She showed herself out, leaving Madison to think about what the other woman had said.

Maybe she was right. Maybe she was going about this the wrong way. Maybe she really was using a microscope and focusing very narrowly when she should be casting a wide net and seeing what she could haul to shore.

Ha! That was easier said than done, but the more she mulled over the idea, the more it felt right. Now all she had to do was figure out what it meant. And then how to go about implementing it.

And she'd better do it soon. Before that slow downward spiral increased its pace, becoming something that no force on earth could stop. Before a child's modest wish list was nothing more than a memory, and a father's last hope was pulverized into dust.

# CHAPTER TWO

SHE WASN'T IN her office.

Theo had knocked and then peeked into the small space before moving inside. He felt a little bit like an interloper, but figured he could as easily wait for her in here as go looking for her. The fact was, he was half-afraid of going to Ivy's room and finding them in a cute little huddle like he had three days ago. Since then he'd forced himself to let Madison alone to do her work. If he hounded her every moment of every day, he would do more harm than good.

Or so he told himself. In reality, he wasn't sure he was ready to face her after his panicked flight the last time. And he wasn't sure why.

He dropped into one of the little chairs, wondering why her office was so spartan when most other doctors' spaces were decked out with squashy leather chairs and the personal touches of its occupants.

It was because this hadn't been an office at all. It had been a supplies cupboard, but it was all they'd had available, since the renovations on Dr. Camargo's office were running behind schedule. But she hadn't offered one word of complaint or acted like they'd set her in a place that was beneath her status. They were damned lucky to have someone like her, and Theo knew it.

He glanced at her desktop, finding it neat and mostly empty except for the stack of file folders on the left-hand side, at the top of which was Ivy's chart. His fingers brushed across the cover, the temptation to open it coming and going. There was nothing in there that she wouldn't have already told him. Then he spotted a small notebook. It was on the right side of the desk toward the back. He was almost sure that was the same notebook she'd tucked into her pocket after her *tête-à-tête* with Ivy. What was in it? Notes about the case?

No, she'd been scratching in that when he'd caught them giggling. They'd been making plans, Madison had said.

About Christmas.

The notebook was on her side of the desk, so he'd have to stretch across to reach it.

*It's not like it's a personal diary, Theo.*

And if it had anything to do with Ivy, didn't he have a right to know what was in it?

His palm slid across the smooth wooden surface of the desk, and he had to lean slightly to reach it. His fingertips landed on the cover, preparing to drag the item toward him, when a slight breeze swept across his nape, sending the hairs rising in attention.

He pulled back in a hurry, turning to face whoever'd entered the room.

Damn.

It was Madison, and she'd caught him red-handed. Well, not really, since he hadn't got a chance to crack the cover on that book.

"Theo, this is a surprise. Were you looking for me?" Her voice was slightly breathless, and she hurried around to the other side of the desk and opened a drawer, sweeping the offending item into it.

There was definitely something in there she didn't want him to see. And that just made him want to look even more.

Dressed in a black cowl-necked sweater that hugged its way from her shoulders to the tops of her slender thighs, it set his senses on high alert. Just like the last time they had been together. He swallowed and tried to regroup and remember his reason for coming here. It certainly hadn't been to ogle her.

"I was, actually. I wanted to know how Naomi fared with Ivy. She told me you changed tack a bit on her therapy. You're no longer actively trying to get her to walk?"

"Not at the moment." She dropped into her office chair and explained her reasoning pretty much the same way Naomi had described the plan to him. And he had to admit he agreed, even if it felt like they were giving ground to some hidden monster—one that was busy pulling a rope from the hidden safety of a screen. It might be out of sight but the effects were apparent to anyone watching the display. They couldn't use brute force to overpower the lurker so they were simply trying to stop it from gaining traction.

"What's our next step?"

"I'm not quite sure. The treatment team is meeting today. I'll digest their findings later."

"I'm aware of the meeting. So what are you bringing to the table?"

"Table? I've been to one or two of the meetings, but wasn't planning on going to today's."

Theo's heart chilled in an instant, even though he'd been the one to say she wasn't required to go to them. "Reason?" Maybe this was where she conceded that she was giving up.

"I wasn't invited."

That made him sit back for a second. "You're always invited. And they'll want you there. *I* want you there. If you're waiting for a formal, gold-foiled envelope to arrive on your desk, that probably isn't going to happen." He forced a smile he hoped reflected reassurance, although it certainly didn't match what was churning around on the inside. What if she decided she wanted to focus on other cases and not spend the bulk of her time on Ivy anymore? Or, worse, what if she'd noticed the tugs of interest he'd felt—even just a minute or two ago—despite his efforts to sweep them under the rug and out of sight? Would she think he was using his position to try to pressure her to prioritize Ivy's treatment above anyone else's?

His instinct as a father was to do exactly that. Help his child in any way he could. Use whatever means he could.

And yet he knew he had to push all of that aside and hold tight to his professional ethics. He'd started this hospital as a way to help people. If he chucked that aside and gave anyone preferential treatment, he would be flying in the face of his convictions.

Madison pulled her hair to the side and let it flow over her shoulder, the golden highlights contrasting with the dark knit of her sweater. And there it was again. That tickle in his midsection that was wreaking havoc with his objectivity.

*Dangerous territory.* Yes, it was. And his earlier thoughts about her trespassing? If he was the one putting out the welcome mat, he could hardly accuse her of wandering where she wasn't invited.

She leaned forward, some of those silky strands of hair brushing across the surface of her desk.

He swallowed again, trying to think of something to say to cover the moment. She beat him to it.

"I know this is going to sound strange, but I've been sending my findings to the group, and they've relayed any information they wanted me to have. It's how I've always worked, even back at my own hospital in the States. I look at all the pieces and try to put them together to form a diagnosis. It's hard for me to do that with a bunch of voices and emotions tangling with each other."

Like the ones going round and round his head right now?

Maybe this was why she wasn't getting on with one or two of the doctors at the hospital. He knew some of those sessions could get heated, with specialists vying for a chance to be heard, but Theo had always thought that was a healthy atmosphere. Hope Hospital emphasized working as treatment teams with the idea that more input was better for the hospital's patients. He was finding out that Madison's file was right. She preferred prowling around the outskirts.

But she was much sought after in the States. So maybe they shouldn't try to stuff her into a box she didn't fit into. Even if Theo himself had created that particular box.

"I understand. And I'll respect that decision. To a degree."

What had happened to not pushing Ivy's needs to the forefront? Or telling her that those meetings were optional?

"I'm sorry? What does that mean?"

"Just that the hospital uses these meetings not only as a chance to bounce around ideas but also to provide accountability to all the players."

"Accountability." Her palms pressed against the surface of the desk, an edge of tension beginning to infuse her words. "As in you don't think I'm carrying my weight here?"

She was getting angry, and hell if he didn't like the little hints of emotion: the sideways tilt of her head, the color sweeping up her cheeks...the way her gaze remained riveted to his face.

Especially that last part.

Damn. So much for keeping this cool and impersonal.

"I phrased that badly. Let's call it curiosity. I would like to know your thoughts on their thoughts. I was hoping to get to that meeting today as well."

Her hands dropped into her lap and the tension seemed to flow out of her.

"I'll be happy to share my thoughts. I just don't want to waste my..." She smiled. "Sorry, badly phrased. I don't want to spend two hours in a chaotic team meeting when I could be looking down other avenues. I promise I do glance over what the team discusses. It just takes me a while to get into my work mode, and having my day cut into pieces with meetings makes it doubly hard, especially if I'm trying to piece together a complicated list of symptoms."

"Understood." Theo, whose days were often "cut into pieces," as she put it, often wished he could just put a "Do Not Disturb" sign on his door and get in eight hours of uninterrupted work. "Would you prefer to just write up your findings and send them to me?"

"I think it would be faster to tell them to you directly, if that's okay. It can be a voicemail, if you're too busy to take my call."

He was never too busy to discuss Ivy. "I'll make time. But if you want to pass on information directly, why don't we set up our own face-to-face meeting of sorts? You tell me the time that works best for you."

"Okay, that's easy. The end of my official work day. Six o'clock or so?" She sat up, so the ends of her hair no longer brushed along the top of her desk. As hard as he tried, he couldn't stop the image of that hair sliding across his skin—skin in an area that was suddenly shifting upward at an alarming rate.

She tossed the offending locks behind her shoulder, going back to that professional demeanor he'd come to recognize, while he struggled to regain control of thoughts that were anything but professional.

"That works for me. I was just getting ready to head down and see Ivy. Do you want to go with me?"

He shouldn't. He should put some distance between them for a while—at least until his strange reaction to her had a chance to power down.

Then his gaze went to the right-hand side of her desk, where that little notebook had sat. Was she taking that with her?

That made his decision. "I haven't checked on her in a couple of hours, so I think I'll join you."

A buzzing came from the other side of the desk and she lifted a finger, asking him to wait. Lifting her cellphone, she looked at the readout and then put the device to her ear. "Dr. Archer here."

She listened to whoever was on the other end of the line, frowning slightly. "And the others?"

Her chest lifted and she expelled an audible sigh. He could fairly see the tension that had gathered in her shoulders. "Okay, thank you for letting me know."

Setting the phone on the desk, she pressed

her fingertips against the surface for several seconds.

"Was that something about Ivy?"

"The test results came back from her Lyme panel."

"And?" He waited, his heart in his chest. Was this the answer they'd been looking for?

"I'm sorry, Theo, but they're negative. All of them. Ivy doesn't have Lyme disease."

Sitting on the side of the bed a half-hour later, listening to her little patient talk about what she'd had for lunch, caused a lump to form in Madison's throat. It looked like Santa was going to have a hard time delivering the first wish on Ivy's list.

Had Theo peeked inside that book before she'd come into the office? She should have written the list somewhere besides the first page, but she'd had no idea at the time that the girl's first request would be something of such a personal nature.

Looking at the stiff way he stood in the corner, watching them, it was hard to imagine him ever liking the holiday, especially since the news they'd been waiting for hadn't materialized. She had pinned her hopes on Lyme disease being the culprit, especially since the symptoms of it were often vague and could appear like those that Ivy had. They were back where they'd started yet again. She should be used to it. And she was. The challenging nature of her work had always energized her.

But not today.

For each terrible disease that was ruled out, another waited in the wings.

And right now Theo looked pretty exhausted, the smile lines around his eyes now tinged with white.

She ached for him. Wished there was something she could say or do that would make this easier.

She'd been surprised to find him in her office earlier. Surprised at the way her heart had jumped to attention.

Was that why she'd agreed to meet him personally to review the details of the case?

*Not smart, Madison.*

There was something about the man that touched a spark within her, though. Maybe it was the brave front he was putting on for his daughter's sake. Or the fact that he'd walked through some hard years, something to which she could relate. She'd struggled through some heartache of her own as a kid. Since reaching adulthood and graduating from medical school, though, things had been smooth sailing.

Sure they had. Because she was on a roll as far as the dating scene went.

Actually, things were pretty dry. Men weren't exactly lining up to go out with a diagnostician. Then again, she wasn't scrambling to go out with them either. Her days had been too full of work and…work. She was busy. Which made the lonely nights a little easier to bear. Right?

Her glance tracked back to Theo, and she swallowed.

"Did you get to see Doodle?" she asked, forcing her thoughts back to Ivy.

Doodle, the labradoodle, had been a regular visitor around the hospital, thanks to Evie, the ICU receptionist who was slated to return to nursing school after the holidays. She'd come up with the idea of bringing in a Pets as Therapy dog. He'd been such a hit with the children that the dog and his handler, Alana, came by most days to visit the different pediatric areas. The family suites were probably some of the last on the list today. But Evie had said the pair would be by soon.

"Yes, this morning. He was so sweet and

nice. I really would love…" Ivy's eyes went to Theo, and then her shoulders slumped. "Oh, well."

Madison's heart cramped. The little girl had almost blurted out that she wanted a dog. Maybe she should have. It was better for Theo to give her a definite answer than for Ivy to pine after something she might never have.

Like the love of a mother?

Madison's breath stalled for a few painful seconds.

Ivy's mom had died, but surely she'd loved her daughter.

That didn't make the loss any easier. But at least she hadn't simply wandered in and out of Ivy's life, until one day she hadn't been there at all—leaving a heartbroken child to wonder what she'd done to make her mother go away.

Was she thinking of Ivy? Or herself?

Madison had done the rounds in various foster homes after her mom had disappeared. Finally, she'd been sent to a group home when she'd been a teenager, where she'd stayed until she'd graduated from high school.

The chaos of moving from place to place had made it hard to develop long-term friendships. Maybe that was why she preferred working on her own. And why colleagues saw her as aloof and unfriendly. She'd relied on herself for so long that she didn't know how to ask for help. Or to trust that someone would catch her if she fell.

"I didn't realize they brought the dog in here." Theo's low voice was neutral. A little too neutral.

"They did, and I loved him so much. He even fell asleep on my bed while I was stroking him." She pulled her covers up to her thin chest. "Do you think Doodle can come and see me again?"

Theo moved from his position against the wall to sit in a chair beside her bed. "I'll have to see how those visits work, exactly, but I think it can be arranged if you would like that."

"Oh, I would!"

Theo glanced at Madison with brows that went up slightly. In accusation? Had Ivy shared with him her desire for a puppy of her own, or...and here went her wandering thoughts once again...had he looked inside that notebook after all? She gave a slight shake of her head to indicate she hadn't put Ivy up to it.

"They've been trying to bring him by to

visit all of the children before Christmas. He's been wearing his elf hat, since he's one of Santa's helpers." She hoped he'd understand what she was trying to say, that they were linking the visits with the man the hospital had hired to play Santa. "I guess it was just Ivy's turn for a special visit."

"I guess it was. An elf, huh?" His voice, like his eyes, had a speculative sound to it. So what if he thought she was behind Doodle's visit or that she was inserting herself where she wasn't welcome? Once they were alone, she would set him straight. Or maybe she would ask Evie to make Ivy a priority and have the labradoodle stop by more often.

Although why she wanted to make him uneasy, she had no idea. A little quid pro quo for the way he hung around in her thoughts—where he most definitely was *not* welcome?

"Yep, an elf. It seems Santa sometimes uses locals to help him do his work."

"And sometimes he uses people from a long way away to do his miracles." The graveled plea behind the words made her tummy twist and turn.

So much for a quid pro quo. Any desire to make him uncomfortable vanished, replaced by a plea of her own.

*Please don't pin all your hopes on me.*

And yet he was. She knew it. Knew he'd called her to come to the hospital because of this very skill set. Normally Madison thrived under that kind of high-pressure atmosphere, the urgency making her job exciting and unpredictable. Her mind seemed to revel in taking a scattered array of seemingly unconnected symptoms and somehow fitting them together.

Only she'd never been colleagues with a parent before. Or connected with a child the way she had with this one.

Her fingers tweaked Ivy's hair and she forced a smile, pretending the wordplay hadn't suddenly become deadly serious. "Miracles can come from many different sources."

"Will Pablo get a miracle?" The little girl glanced up at her.

Madison saw Theo go still at the mention of the little boy diagnosed with muscular dystrophy who'd been a couple of doors down from Ivy's room until they'd moved him to PICU.

Madison swallowed. "Pablo left today." She tried to put enough subtle emphasis on the word "left" that Theo would realize she wasn't talking about going home.

A muscle went to work in his jaw, pulsing a couple of times before going quiet. He got it.

He lowered himself into a nearby chair, elbows on his knees, head down.

Thinking about how Pablo could just as easily have been his daughter?

Unwilling to leave him to figure out a way to respond to Ivy's question about miracles—or the lack thereof—Madison spoke up. "Why don't we see if we can challenge your dad to a game of Go Fish?"

Up came Theo's head, eyes fixed on her. "Go Fish?"

Those two words had never sounded as elegant as they did in that accent of his. It forced a smile from her.

"It's a card game that uses a special deck." She never knew what kind of cases she might be called in on, so she'd gotten used to carrying a pack in one of her pockets. Sometimes getting someone's mind off an illness helped calm nerves, whether it be children, parents, or anyone else. She'd been kind of famous for producing that deck of cards at her hospital in the U.S., had often being called on to help calm a child who was being prepared for sur-

gery. It was the one time she'd felt wanted—
needed—for something other than her skills
at diagnosis.

"I know what it is. I'm just not sure how
you're going to manage—"

Out came the pack of cards. Theo's head
gave a funny little tilt as if he couldn't believe his eyes.

"Now I've seen everything." His glance
landed on her. "Madison the magician."

The way he'd said that…

A shiver rolled over her that she did her
best to suppress.

"It's good therapy for cognitive and fine
motor skills."

And it gave Madison a way to observe her
patients, looking for any tiny changes that she
might miss otherwise. If she played a quick
game over a period of a couple of weeks—or
months—she could see disease progression.
The first game gave her a base from which
to compare progress or deterioration. In this
case, she prayed she wouldn't see the latter.

She let the magician comment stand, instead of going into that kind of explanation.
Maybe later.

Nodding at the spot on the bed next to her,
she said, "Move closer, Doc, so I can deal."

There was a moment's hesitation, but he finally got up and sat on the mattress, watching as she dealt the first hand and placed the rest of the deck face down between them. She hoped he didn't see the slight tremor in her hand as she did so.

Although she'd come prepared to play, Theo's presence was threatening to derail her. And although she'd invited him to sit next to her, she was now wishing she hadn't. She was hyper-aware of everything about him. His scent. The way the fingers of his left hand rested on his thigh.

The way he was avoiding looking at her.

Lordy. She was in trouble.

When dealing with children, she sometimes adopted rather goofy voices as a way to make her patients laugh. Ha! There was no way she was going to do that today.

Ivy picked up her hand, although it took some effort to do so. The little girl's struggle poured an icy dose of reality over her. Madison tensed, resisting the urge to offer help, and when Theo looked like he might intervene, she spoke up. "She can do it. Let her."

"Yeah, Daddy, I can do it." She carefully separated her cards, fumbling a little and dropping one of them in the process. There was silence as she recovered and picked it up again.

"Player to the left of the dealer goes first." She would have had Ivy go first, no matter which side she'd been on.

The girl's eyes swiveled between the two of them before focusing on her father. "Do you have any threes, Daddy?"

Theo handed over a card. "I have one."

Ivy's grin lit up the room. "I knew it." She asked for another card, this time from Madison, who didn't have the requested item. Then it was Theo's turn.

"Madison, do you have any aces?"

"Go fish."

He didn't move for a second. "How about up your sleeve? Do you have any there?"

She froze as his eyes finally met hers. Nerve endings crackled as she stared back at him.

"Daddy! That would be cheating, and Madison doesn't do that."

Madison snapped her gaze back to her cards, none of the numbers coming into focus.

She would cheat in a heartbeat if it meant outsmarting whatever was going on inside Ivy's small body.

It took them fifteen minutes to declare

Theo the winner, and to Madison it seemed like an eternity. All she wanted to do was retreat to the safety of her office, lay her head down on her desk and try to come up with some kind of answer. For Ivy. And, heaven help her, for her father.

Especially after seeing slivers of change in Ivy over the course of the game. Her cards appeared to get heavier and heavier, the young girl having to set them down in between hands. But her mind was as sharp as ever. In fact, she seemed to make up for her deteriorating condition by memorizing what was in her hand. And when she said, "Go fish," without even looking, neither Madison nor Theo challenged her. By the end the girl was yawning, even though it was only six in the early evening.

"Tired, kiddo?" she asked.

"No."

Theo gathered the cards into a neat stack then leaned over to kiss his daughter's head. "Why don't you rest for a little while, and I'll help Dr. Archer put these away, okay?"

"Will you tell me a story later?"

"Of course."

Ivy lay back against her pillows, her face pale, the muscles in her thin arms lax and still. She made no move to hug her dad. Or wave goodbye. For a child who was normally so affectionate, it struck a chord of fear in Madison.

If she felt it, then that chord had to be a million clanging gongs going off in Theo's head.

God, why couldn't she figure this out?

A hot wave of nausea seared up her esophagus as she pictured Theo tucked in next to his child, reading her a bedtime story.

How many stories did she have until that bed was empty? Just like Pablo's.

Twenty? Ten?

Two?

The pain grew, engulfing her with a terrible sense of responsibility.

She needed to fix a picture of that bed in her head and stare at it. Force herself to get to grips with the reality that this was life or death.

*Wasted time can't be recaptured.* Hadn't she just said that not very long ago? Yes, and it was true. It couldn't.

Neither could lost opportunities.

She straightened her backbone. So she needed to do something about it. Needed to work faster. Harder.

Theo led the way from the room and handed her the rest of the cards. "I gather there was a reason for that. Quite clever, actually."

It took her a few seconds to realize he hadn't read her thoughts but was talking about the game.

She drew a careful breath, trying to tamp down the chaotic emotions that had been racing through her a few seconds ago. "I wondered if you would figure it out."

"Only after I caught those eagle eyes studying Ivy as she played. After the third or fourth time it hit me that you were monitoring her." He sighed. "She's getting tired more quickly."

"Yes."

"What else?"

"Theo..."

He shook his head. "I want to know."

And he deserved to. She just didn't want to be the one to tell him. But she owed it to him to be honest.

"Her arms have developed a tremor when holding them in front of her." Muscle wasting from lack of use. The problem was, no one had any idea what was causing them to atrophy. "By the time we were ready to leave the room she was completely spent. I have a feeling she forced herself to keep going. For you."

"Hell."

Theo put his hands behind his neck and stretched his arms out to the side. A pop sounded in one of his joints, the sharp sound making her flinch slightly.

"Sorry. Bad habit."

She could understand that. She had her little quirks as well. But they were more along the lines of insomnia when she was dealing with a puzzling case. She'd had more than her share of nights doodling symptoms on a whiteboard and looking for something that would ring a bell. Ivy's symptoms were plastered on a board she'd propped in the dining room of her apartment. And she had definitely spent more than one sleepless night searching for a clue.

"Her treatment team wants to do more blood tests," he said.

"I know. I asked that the report be sent down. The list of what it's not is growing longer, which is good in that the list of what it could be is getting shorter."

"Is it?" His arms went back to his sides. "How long can she go on like this? At some point it's going to reach a point of no return."

Hadn't she thought something very similar moments earlier?

Fighting through the catch in her throat, she turned toward him, wrapping her fingers tightly around his wrist. She wasn't sure if she was clutching him to reassure herself or to lend weight to what she was about to say.

"Hey. We're not there yet. She's still breathing." *Not* the best way to word it. She hurried to add, "The weakness is only in her limbs and hips at the moment."

"Thank God for that." The second he reached up to cover her hand with his, she knew touching him had been a big mistake. The heat from his skin was electric, unseen calluses scraping across her nerve endings and bringing them to life.

She should move. Tug her hand free. But since she'd initiated the contact, she had no one to blame but herself.

"I'll take as many of those 'at the moments' as I can get," he murmured. "Until we can figure this out."

The hallway was completely empty. There were fewer people staying in this section over the holidays, since everyone who could go home to be with their families did.

Ivy could probably have a great team of

caregivers if she went home as well, but Theo wanted her here. Near him. They had an amazing bond. One she'd never had, growing up.

A tightness in her chest warned her that her emotions were venturing far too close to the surface.

She glanced up and caught him staring at her. She wanted to promise him miracles and happy endings and anything else he was looking for. But she couldn't. "Sometimes we just have to do our living in those moments."

"Yes. I agree."

The seconds stretched into minutes. Neither of them moved. Until—real or imagined—his thumb brushed the back of her hand.

Her body erupted instantly, nipples drawing tight inside her thin bra. God, she hoped he couldn't see them. Hoped he couldn't—

"Madison…"

A sharp *ping!* signaled the arrival of the elevator. Jerking free, she took a hurried step back. Then another, struggling to catch her breath.

She needed to escape while she could. "I'll see you tomorrow for our meeting."

"And another game of cards?"

"Cards?" Her brain was a huge mudslide of buried thoughts and emotions at the moment, and so it took her a second for the words to make sense. "Oh. You don't have to be here for that, if you don't want to."

The less contact she had with him the better. At least it was looking that way. What had she been thinking?

She hadn't been.

Evidently neither had he, if his response to her living-in-those-moments comment was any indication. It had certainly veered away from the professional and into the personal.

Her lack of dating life had shown its ugly face. She'd lapped up the attention like a lovesick teenager.

"I'd like to be, if it's okay. It gives me a chance to measure her abilities as well."

Two people stepped off the elevator, one of them giving Theo a wave that asked him to wait before heading toward them.

Madison did not want to hang around. Her face was already burning. Someone was sure to notice, since she had the worst poker face in history. Theo seemed to be thinking the same thing. "I'll see you tomorrow. Call me when you know a time."

"Okay."

And with that, she fled down the hall in the opposite direction of the approaching staff members. It would take her longer to get back to her little cubicle this way, but she didn't care. Right now, all she was worried about was how she was going to face Ivy's father tomorrow. Or keep herself from doing something else stupid. Like hurtling down a road that led from professional courtesy toward unprofessional crush.

# CHAPTER THREE

"WE WOULD LIKE to congratulate Naomi Collins on moving in with Finn Morgan. He is one lucky devil."

Madison, who'd been talking to Naomi about Ivy, saw the woman's eyes widen in surprise as the voice continued over the hospital PA system.

"Oh, my God," the physical therapist muttered. "Is that Finn?"

Madison's lips curled in a smile. She knew Finn and Naomi were an item, but had had no idea their relationship had progressed to this point. "It certainly sounds like him."

"He said he wanted to keep it under wraps."

That made her laugh. "Well, he's evidently changed his mind."

"So it would appear. That man has some explaining to do." Naomi didn't sound angry, though. She sounded…in love. Completely and madly in love.

And the fact that Finn was announcing to the world that they had moved in together? It was dreamy in a way Madison had never experienced. The quick fumbling in the back of her prom date's car had been anything but a dream. It had left her feeling empty and confused. And the guy had never called her for another date, something that had hurt almost as much as her mother's abandonment. She'd been wary of relationships ever since.

So why was Theo affecting her the way he was?

She glanced at Naomi. She didn't seem empty. Or confused. She seemed very, very sure of what she wanted. And what she wanted was Finn.

And that, my dear, was love. The kind that real dreams were made of. The kind she'd never found.

"Congratulations, honey." She gave her new friend a quick hug. "If anyone deserves this, you do."

Naomi waved a hand in front of her face. "Stop or you'll make me cry. Or he'll make me cry. Or someone will."

"I'd go find him if I were you, before he

adds to his story and says something really embarrassing."

"Good idea." She gave Madison's arm a quick squeeze. "Can we continue this another time?"

"Of course. Go."

With that, Naomi hurried down the corridor in the direction of the elevators.

Madison watched her go until she disappeared into a small group of people.

What would it be like to find someone like Finn and settle down?

She wasn't likely to ever settle down, wasn't sure she even knew how to stay in one place longer than a few months or a year. Even her job changed repeatedly. Well, not the job itself. Just where she practiced it. She seemed to gravitate toward the hardest of the hard cases. Her last hospital had been different in that regard. She'd been there for two years. And now she wasn't. But she'd left there expecting to go back. Hadn't she?

Or had coming to England put something into motion that felt both familiar and unsettling? Like pulling up her tent stakes and wandering to a new city with new faces and new challenges.

Was she really bored so easily?

Or was she too afraid to get attached, expecting what was familiar to be yanked away from her at any moment?

Like her prom date? Or her mother's love? Or all those foster homes she'd lived in?

One thing was for sure. No one would be announcing she'd moved in with them over a hospital intercom. She'd made sure of it.

The universe had tricked her one too many times. She no longer wanted to play the relationship version of Go Fish. There was no card out there that matched hers.

She swallowed, not liking her train of thought. She was single because she chose to be single, not for any other reason. She certainly didn't need to be looking for wisdom in a child's card game. Time to go back to her little cubicle and lose herself in Ivy's case or someone else's.

Once there, she sat behind the desk and opened the drawer that contained the little notebook she was using for Ivy. Flipping open the cover, she saw that infamous list again. Her pen paused in front of the first item and stared at it for a moment or two. Then she drew two straight slash lines underneath the words *Make Daddy like Christmas*.

Maybe while Santa was at it he could figure out why she had just as much of a problem with this season as Theo did. Maybe even more. But until then, she would just keep chugging along until all the baubles, trees and Go Fish games were packed away and life became normal again.

Theo pushed off the couch in his office and dragged his hand through his hair, trying to bring to mind the positive affirmation the hospital chaplain was always going on about. What was it?

Today was a new day, with new hope and new possibilities. Don't dwell on days past.

Which day was that? The day when Hope had died, taking joy and love with her? Or the more recent one where he'd put his hand over that of another woman for the first time in a very long time?

Madison had done something his late wife had loved to do to get his attention when confronting an important matter. She would wrap her fingers around his wrist and grip it tightly. The second the diagnostician had done that it had triggered an automatic response. Only it hadn't been his wife's hand his had reached to cover. It had been Madison's. And within seconds Theo had been acutely aware that he wasn't touching a ghost but flesh and blood. She was warm and alive, her touch reaching inside him and coaxing something to life. Something he'd thought long dead.

His gaze had scoured Madison's face, looking for something. Her cheeks had blushed bright red, something Hope's had never done. And Theo had liked it, had found his attention drifting toward her lips. And then he'd said something stupid. And when her blush had deepened, he'd known he was going to kiss her.

The sudden arrival of the elevator had broken the spell.

Thank God.

He and Hope had been colleagues as well as lovers. And good friends. And she'd put her career on hold for him, something he now regretted bitterly. He didn't regret Ivy's birth. Or the hospital's founding—Hope had been just as excited about that as he'd been.

No, he regretted neglecting her. Putting both of their lives on pause while he'd pursued his dream. And, yes, the hospital did good work. But had it been worth sacrificing a part of his life he could never get back?

He would never know.

What if Madison decided to leave the hospital because of what he'd done? He'd taken a friendly gesture on her part and read something into it. Or had he? Either way, he'd turned it into something more.

He couldn't afford to have her pack up and take off. Even though she hadn't come up with a solution to whatever was happening with Ivy, he had a feeling that she would. Or at the very least she would put them on the right track. And if he'd ruined that out of some maudlin trip down memory lane...

No, it had been more than that. Within seconds of touching her he'd been acutely aware that it had been Madison he'd been touching and not Hope. And hadn't wanted to break that contact. Had wanted it to go on.

Was it about sex? It had been a long time since he'd been with anyone. But even if it was just a physical reaction, then of all people for that to happen with...

He needed to find her and set things right, if possible. And if she hadn't even been aware that sparks were igniting inside him?

He'd just be subtle about it. *Really?* He wasn't exactly known for his subtlety. Hope had often rolled her eyes at him because he pretty much said what he thought. He'd tempered that in later years, learning that to run a hospital took more than a bull-in-a-china-shop approach. So he'd learned tact. Of a sort.

Madison was supposed to meet him to discuss Ivy's treatment and to play cards.

Hell, since when had his duties included playing children's games?

Since his daughter had become ill, that's when. And he respected Madison's ingenuity in assessing her condition without making Ivy uncomfortable. She'd made it fun. And he was damned glad of it.

Hmm. Madison was supposed to set up a time to meet with him. He glanced at his watch. It was still early, just before six a.m. There was time to go down to the hospital cafeteria and grab a bite for him and Ivy and figure out his strategy. Maybe he would gauge the diagnostician's behavior and decide whether he needed to address the issue or not.

And if she blushed again?

He would damn well keep his hands to himself.

A few minutes later he was balancing a tray containing a bowl of warm porridge, fruit and a French omelet and headed back to the elevator, trying to push the button inside with an elbow.

"Need some help?"

He glanced up to find the very person he'd been thinking about standing just inside the doors. Not a trace of red graced her face, and her voice was as steady as the day was long. Maybe he'd overreacted. "I was just taking some breakfast up to Ivy."

"That's an awful lot of food for one little girl." Up went her brows.

He smiled, his insides relaxing. "I was planning on joining her. Ivy hates eggs." He nodded at his own plate, where the clear cover revealed its contents.

"Ah, so she has the oatmeal and fruit?"

He smiled at the American term for porridge. "Yes, she loves...um...oatmeal."

"She has good taste." Madison pressed the button for the fourth floor and the elevator headed up. She didn't push a second button.

"Were you going to her room as well?"

"Not until a little later, but I wanted to talk to you."

Oh, hell. Maybe he hadn't overreacted. Was this where she said she was catching the next flight out?

"Something with Ivy?"

"No. I wanted to apologize for getting too personal outside her room."

It was then he realized that her voice was a little too steady and her face was not only *not* blushing, it was deadly pale. And her hands were clasped behind her back where he couldn't see them.

What kind of irony was that? He'd been worried sick about how his behavior had come across, and here she was worrying about her own.

"I was upset and you were trying to reassure me. Nothing more. Nothing less."

It sounded ridiculous. And a little bit condescending. He also wasn't happy with the fact that he hadn't admitted to his own part in what had happened. It would be a whole lot easier to let her take the blame and leave it at that, but it didn't sit right. It was time to set the record straight. "If anyone needs to apologize it's me. I actually woke up this morning worried that you might have thought I was being too forward yesterday. But, again, I was upset. And concerned."

"I know. Really I do." Her hands came out from behind her back, and at first he thought she was going to touch him again, and had to force himself to stand still. All she did, though, was reposition the porridge container, which had slid a little too close to the edge of the tray.

"Thank you. I appreciate that. I wouldn't want to do anything that would…" He gave a half-shrug.

Her head tilted. "That would what?"

"Make you leave the hospital." There. He'd said it. His biggest fear was laid out for both of them to see.

"I'm not going to leave. Not yet. So if you're afraid I won't help with Ivy's case anymore, you can rest easy." Her brows went up. "I've dealt with worried dads before."

That made him frown. "You've had men make passes at you before?"

There was a moment or two of silence as she stared at him. "Is that what you were doing?"

Hell, he hadn't meant to say that. And he actually hadn't got to the pass part yesterday, although it had definitely been on his mind.

The doors to the elevator opened as he was casting around for something to say. They both stepped off and into the corridor, where Theo stopped and faced her.

"Not exactly. I forgot who I was with for a second."

She blinked. "I'm sorry?"

"Hell, I'm mucking this up completely. Let's just say I shouldn't have done what I did. And it won't happen again."

He needn't have worried, if her expression was anything to go by. He'd probably just earned himself a knee to the groin if he even looked in her direction ever again.

"Then we're both agreed. We were both worried about Ivy and not acting the way we would normally."

"Yes, that's it exactly."

And if she wanted to believe he had been thinking of Hope that whole time, it would be easier on everyone. Including him.

"I'll help you get her breakfast situated. I want to peek in on her anyway."

"No card games this morning?"

"I'll be back a little later to play, once I've checked on my other patients."

That's right. It was too easy to forget that Madison wasn't at this hospital solely for him and Ivy. His mind scrambled around a bit before rephrasing that internal thought. She wasn't here solely for Ivy. She'd been flown in because the hospital's own diagnostician had suddenly been offered a six-month medical mission to Africa and had left unexpectedly. Dr. Camargo had been texted about Ivy's case a couple of months ago, but he was just as stumped as everyone else. He was the one who'd suggested bringing in another set of eyes. Thankfully Madison had agreed to come.

His phone vibrated in his pocket. Reaching for it with the tray still in his hand, he glanced at the screen. "That's strange."

Motioning to her to wait a second before going into his daughter's room, he pressed the talk button and put the phone to his ear. "Hawkwood here."

"Theo, this is Marco. We've got a couple of cases down here we could use your help on, if your surgeon's hands are still up to the task."

It was very unusual for them to call him in on anything nowadays, so this had to be urgent. "Alice?"

Marco Ricci and his fiancée Alice Baxter were both pediatric surgeons and handled a lot of the general surgeries in the hospital.

"She's tied up with an appendicitis case right now, and I need to scrub in on a suspected ovarian torsion."

Both of those were medical emergencies. "Okay, what do you need help with?"

"We have an eighteen-month-old who is

also presenting with right side lower quadrant pain, fever and vomiting."

"Another appendicitis?"

"We thought so at first because of the location. But the scans actually show a probable intussusception. Ryan is doing a heart cath right now, so we're running out of available surgeons."

"Air enema?"

"Already tried it."

"Okay, I'm on it." A fairly straightforward surgery, intussusception was where part of the intestines telescoped in on itself, causing blockage and restricted blood flow. Timing was critical, since the sooner they could free the affected bowel the better the prognosis.

He pressed the phone against his hip to mute it. "Are you interested in scrubbing in on a surgical case? Suspected intussusception in a toddler. We're running out of surgeons."

"Of course. I'd be happy to help."

"Thanks." Putting the phone back to his ear, he said, "On my way. Dr. Archer will assist."

"Great. Tell her thank you."

"I already have. What suite?"

"Seven is open. I think it's been cleaned up after the last case."

"I'll check on it. Get back to your patient. We've got it from here."

He rang off and after putting Ivy's food in front of her Theo left his own on the counter for later. They hurried back to the elevator, arriving at the second floor—where all the surgical suites were located—ten minutes later. Theo went to the desk. "Intestinal intussusception patient? We're here to scrub in."

The young woman's eyes widened. "Right away, Mr. Hawkwood. Let me just check for you."

He frowned. He hated how his position caused some people to treat him differently than other doctors. Yes, he was the CEO of the hospital, but he was also a doctor...would always be a doctor. His inheritance hadn't changed any of that.

A minute later, the nurse came back. "They're getting her prepped for surgery."

"Great, I'd like to take a look at the contrast scans if I could."

"Of course. Here's her chart number." She wrote it on a sheet of paper, handing it over to him. Was it his imagination or had she just batted her lashes at him?

*Your imagination, Theo. You're seeing things that don't exist.*

"This is Dr. Archer. She'll be scrubbing in as well."

Madison reached over to shake the woman's hand with a murmured greeting, then they both headed toward the small conference area to access the computer. A few seconds later they were looking at Meghan Pitruscki's scans. Madison found it first with an exclaimed, "There!" as she pointed to the computer monitor.

The area was in the lower right quadrant, just as Marco had said. "We'll have to get in there to see how compromised the intestines in that area are."

"Once we get them separated they might be fine."

"We can hope." He switched the computer off. "Ready?"

"Yes. It's been a while since I scrubbed in on a surgery so I don't know how much help I'll be."

"Right now, another set of eyes is exactly what I need." Those were almost exactly the same words Dr. Camargo had used when suggesting they bring another diagnostician in.

He'd have surgical nurses to assist, but he'd like Madison there to make sure he didn't miss anything. It had been a while since he'd scrubbed in on a surgery as well.

Once they got the call that the patient was prepped and waiting, they gloved up, Theo using his shoulder to push through the door that led to the surgical suite. The patient lay on a table, her tiny body barely taking up any of its length. The anesthesiologist was already at her head, monitoring the sedation. Theo would meet with her parents after surgery, which was how he preferred it. It was hard to remain objective in the face of anguished pleas and tears. Hell, it was hard to remain objective under the best of circumstances. Somehow operating on a toddler was so much more difficult than treating an adult. There was so much life they hadn't yet got to experience.

Like Ivy?

Nope, not the time to be thinking of his daughter or her problems right now.

"Hello, everyone. Let's get started, shall we?"

Making the first incision with Madison standing beside him, he called out his movement, step by step for the overhead recorder.

Then he was inside the abdominal cavity, carefully making his way through myriad folds of intestines, laying them aside as he continued to search for the affected area. "I see it."

"I do as well," Madison said. "It's red and inflamed, but I don't see evidence of necrotic tissue at this point. We'll know more once you're able to free the trapped portion."

Carefully checking for tears or perforations that could contaminate the abdominal cavity and cause peritonitis, he used his gloved fingers to try to ease the telescoped part out of the confined area. It didn't budge.

The surgical nurse on the other side moved closer, handing over forceps when he asked for them. He tried again.

"It's not coming loose." The intestines were small and slick and, since he was having to be delicate in handling them, he was stumped. "I may have to resection the affected portion." It was a small enough piece that it shouldn't affect little Meghan's digestion, but cutting and removing bowel always carried an added risk. He tried again, using a tiny bit more pressure, but it was still wedged tight.

Madison's low voice whispered past his ear. "Can you try getting some saline in the space between the two and moistening it? Maybe it's adhered."

It was a good idea.

Without needing to be asked, the nurse loaded a syringe with the solution and placed it in his hand. Theo then nudged the plastic tip into the space and slowly pushed the plunger. He made his way around the area, centimeter by centimeter, until he reached his starting point. He handed the syringe back to the nurse, then repeated the separation attempt. This time the trapped portion of the intestine popped free. Theo heard audible sighs of relief come from various parts of the room.

The affected tissue was blue from lack of oxygen, but hopefully they'd caught it before it went necrotic. He'd give it a few minutes before closing up to make sure. In the meantime, he felt along the length to make sure there wasn't another section that they'd missed.

"It's pinking up." Madison's voice broke through. He finished his inspection, though, before going back to look. It was indeed returning to the pale pink of the rest of the intestines.

"It looks good. Thanks, people, great work today," he called out to everyone in the room.

Returning everything to the abdominal cavity, he glanced up. "Let's get her closed up and back home for Christmas, where she belongs."

Over the next twenty minutes he sutured muscle and skin and then placed a layer of sterile gauze over the area, taping it in place. Meghan would have a little war wound on her lower belly, but that was much better than the alternative.

"Done." He nodded to the anesthesiologist. "Let's wake our little patient up."

"Gladly."

When he glanced at Madison, the corners of her eyes had crinkle lines and she nodded at him. "Thanks for asking me to come."

He should be the one thanking her. She was the one who'd suggested he try saline to lubricate the tissues. It had worked beautifully.

"Thank you, you were a big help."

"Just glad to work on something that is a little more straightforward."

"Something other than Ivy?"

"No, of course not. It's just different from what I normally do."

He shut his eyes for a moment. Why the hell was he putting words into her mouth?

Moving up to the girl's head, he watched as the other doctor adjusted the dials that would send oxygen to her body, replacing the gases that had been used to keep her under sedation.

Twenty minutes later the trach tube had been removed and the toddler's eyes flickered, pure blue irises struggling to focus on his face. He put his hand on her forehead. "Hi, sweetheart. Welcome back."

And just like that it was over and people were moving to do their jobs, and Meghan was wheeled away to the recovery area to finish waking up.

"I need to speak to her parents. Can you wait for me?"

"Of course. How about if I meet you in my office?"

Her tone didn't sound as sure as it had a few minutes ago. Afraid of being alone with him? Well, she should be. Although he'd kept his mind on surgery as it had been happening, now that it was over he found himself wanting to study her, from those cute little smile lines all the way to how her hair drifted in different directions when freed of its normal clip.

Except her hair was covered by a surgical cap at the moment, so there was no hair to see. Just those beautiful clear green eyes and the straight length of her nose. High cheekbones. Smooth forehead. All things he had no business noticing.

"Thanks, I'll try not to be long."

Turning, he forced himself to stride away, ruing the fact that he'd asked her to wait for him. To talk about Ivy's case. That was all. Otherwise he would while away the hours worrying about every little detail of her condition. Better to just talk about it and be done with it. Maybe in the same way that two pairs of eyes had been better than one, two minds might be able to figure out a solution when his was stuck in limbo. A fearful limbo that was stealing his soul just like the disease that was stealing his daughter's ability to move. He had no idea which side would succumb first. His soul. Or his daughter.

*"The symptoms look like appendicitis. But it's not. It's something completely different."*

Theo's words as they'd walked down to the

surgical suite a couple of hours ago stuck in her head and wouldn't leave.

*It looks like appendicitis. But it's not.*

A tickling at the back of her brain was slowly gaining strength. Slowly consuming her other thoughts.

Reaching into her desk, she grabbed her little notebook, flipping a couple of pages past Ivy's wish list, and wrote down her thoughts.

"Add to whiteboard at home: It looks like appendicitis. But it's not."

She didn't know what they meant. Not yet. But she knew from experience that her brain would be fiddling with those words in the background, much like a computer program might work behind the scenes until you opened it again and saw what had happened.

She just hoped it wasn't another rabbit hole.

A quick knock, and then Theo poked his head in. "Thanks."

"I was tempted to go on up to check on Ivy, but I did this instead." She nodded at some food on the desk. "Hope that was okay."

She'd stopped by the cafeteria and bought some fruit for herself and another omelet for Theo, since the one he'd left upstairs had to be stone-cold by now. "I wasn't sure what you had in it, so I just had them add some cheese and seasonings."

His brows went up. "You didn't have to do that."

She smiled. "I know I didn't, but since I was getting something for myself anyway, it only made sense. I called upstairs, and Ivy ate most of her oatmeal and all her fruit. How were Meghan's parents?"

"Relieved. Thanks to you and your saline idea."

"There was no guarantee it would work. It was pure luck."

"It was thinking outside the box." He lowered himself into one of the metal chairs with a groan. "I need to find you some better furniture."

"It's fine. I won't be here forever."

The reminder was more for herself than anything. She was feeling a little too comfortable in her tiny little space, metal chairs and all. Only she didn't want to feel comfortable here. This had never been intended to be permanent.

"I'm aware of that."

There was a hint of something in his tone that made her take a second look. Was he thinking about Ivy and how she might not be here long enough for them to come up with a diagnosis?

She wanted to find a solution as much as he did. Madison did not like leaving things undone. She liked everything tied up with a neat bow, unlike her childhood where things had never been neat and had rarely ever been followed through to completion. Those insecure years had turned her into a fanatic about finishing tasks and making sure she had closure. One way or another.

And closure with Ivy and her dad? What would that look like? She had no idea.

She pushed the plate containing his omelet across to him, placing a fork on top of it. "I'm not leaving until we figure this thing out, Theo, if that's what you're worried about."

His eyes closed for a second. "Sorry. I haven't been getting much sleep lately."

"I can imagine. But you can't help her if you're completely run down yourself."

His hands went behind his neck, and she braced herself for the popping of that shoulder joint. It didn't come as he seemed to catch himself just in time. "I forgot that you don't like that."

How did he even know that? Was she that obvious?

Lord, she hoped not, because that might mean he saw a whole lot more than she wanted him to.

"It's not that I dislike it. It just surprised me that first time. Go ahead if it helps."

"I can do it later. When you're not around." Then he smiled before his eyes tracked to the desk and his head tilted before he opened his box and cut into his omelet. "What are you writing?"

For a split second she thought she'd left the book open to Ivy's wish list, but then remembered what she'd been doing. "I was writing down something that struck me during Meghan's surgery. I'm just not sure why yet."

"You're not sure why it struck you, or why you wrote it down?"

"Both."

She turned the book to face him so he could read it.

"I don't understand."

"Neither do I. Yet. It might mean nothing. Or it could trigger a thought."

He took a bite, his strong throat contracting as he swallowed. "About Ivy's case?"

"Yes, I think so." She felt the need to warn him. "I do this a lot with cases. Many times, it ends up being a dead end. But there are enough times that it's not to keep me doing it."

"You think Ivy's symptoms could be something related to appendicitis?"

"No. I'm not sure why it seemed important. I have a board at the apartment with all Ivy's symptoms on it. It helps me visualize what's happening inside a patient. And if it's staring me in the face at every turn, it can help a diagnosis leap out of nowhere. I'm going to add this to that board."

"You have one made up for Ivy?"

"I do."

They ate in silence for a minute or two, and Madison wished she'd gone ahead and eaten before he'd arrived. Because this companionable silence was disconcerting. It didn't feel as awkward as it should have. In fact, it felt kind of good to be able to sit and talk through a problem with someone. Which was also weird. She usually preferred to work alone, not sharing details with anyone, which was another reason she was loath to go to the meetings upstairs. She preferred to keep her cluttered thoughts to herself. Adding someone else's to the mix was just too confusing. Oh, she could sit and listen to others' ideas, but she rarely wrote them down or added them to her lists. Theo's comment had been the exception to that rule, evidently.

"I'd like to see your board."

She froze. "What?"

"The board you've worked up about Ivy."

Suddenly she was backtracking like crazy. "It's just a mishmash of symptoms." The idea of having Theo in her home threw her into a panic, and she wasn't sure why. She'd had other visitors and it hadn't seemed like a big deal. Hadn't she just wondered about what that closure would look like? If she complicated it by allowing him to walk around her home…

"I know, but I've seen the rest of the team's thoughts and ideas. But not yours."

Yes, he had. "I've talked you through them."

"I'd like to see what you've written down. The order and placement."

"Why?"

"I don't know. But it's important to me. Is it a problem?"

Yes. It was. But there was no way she was going to say that to him.

"If you really think it will help." She was not stupid enough to keep the list from him if he insisted on seeing it. And she could understand being so desperate for any clue that you would do anything to find one.

She'd done that with her birth mom, gone through all kinds of hoops and verbal gymnastics with bureaucrats until she'd discovered a truth she hadn't wanted to find.

But find it she had. And once she'd opened that box, there had been no closing it. She would have preferred to think her mom was out there somewhere, maybe even looking for the child she'd abandoned all those years ago.

She took a deep breath and threw out one more feeble attempt at self-preservation. "I could always take a picture of the board and send it to you."

"If you don't want me in your house, I'll understand."

"It's not that…" It was that. Exactly that. Only there was no way she was going to admit it. "I just didn't want you to drive all that way to look at something that won't make sense to anyone except me."

"I would like a picture for the team, if that's okay, but I'd also like to see it in person, if you don't mind."

"Of course." Now that she'd admitted to having the board at home, she was a little embarrassed for anyone but her to see it in all its chaotic glory. "But I'm warning you, they've already mentioned almost everything that's on there."

He nodded at the notebook as he finished the last bite of his omelet. "Not things like that."

"My brain doesn't always work in an orderly fashion. It could just as easily be erased by tomorrow morning."

"Understood. I actually came by to see when to meet you in Ivy's room."

"I'm just going to play cards with her. Are you sure you want to be roped into that?"

"I'm not being 'roped' into it. Anything that can give insight into what's happening to her will be welcomed with open arms."

"Okay, then let's plan on dinnertime. Unless you need to go home before that."

"I've been sleeping in her room to stay close to her, so that's fine. My housekeeper's bringing me fresh clothes periodically."

Housekeeper. Okay. She knew he was wealthy, since he'd been the one to open the hospital, but evidently he had a lot more money than she'd realized. That explained his comment about the lack of luxurious chairs in her office. Well, she'd grown up at the opposite end of the spectrum and tended to be pretty frugal in a lot of ways. So those metal chairs were just her style. She wasn't poor anymore, per se, but she still didn't like to waste money. So her apartment here was spartan. Just like her apartment back in the States.

Oh, well, he could take it or leave it. She certainly wasn't going to apologize for her taste in decor.

And now that the decision had been made, she was kind of anxious to see his reaction to the space she'd carved out for herself. Would he turn his nose up like some kind of aristocrat?

That didn't seem to match the man she was learning more and more about. But you never could tell. Actions could be deceiving.

Like her own actions yesterday in front of Ivy's room? She'd said it had meant nothing but in her heart of hearts she knew she was deceiving not only him but herself. She was attracted to him.

Only like the anesthesia that had been administered to Meghan before her surgery, she'd better find a way to reverse it. And fast. Or she was setting herself up for a whole lot of heartache.

# CHAPTER FOUR

"Mummy died and went to heaven."

The bald words floating from his daughter's room stopped Theo in his tracks. Delayed almost an hour by an emergency meeting of the board, he could hear the sound of cards being shuffled. There was a pause before it resumed.

"I know she did. But she would be awfully proud of the big girl you've grown into."

A hard lump formed in Theo's throat and his fingers curled into his palms, biting deep. Ivy hadn't mentioned her mother in over a year. It had been last year at Christmas, actually, when she'd asked him if Hope was opening up presents in heaven and if God was like Santa Claus. He'd been hard-pressed to answer those questions so he'd redirected her the best he could and had buried his own heartache deep inside his chest, hoping she couldn't see it.

"Daddy still gets sad sometimes."

"We all get sad sometimes." Another ruffle of cards being shuffled hard. "My mommy is in heaven too."

Madison's mother had died as well? Something about the matter-of-fact way she'd said that made the hair lift on the back of his neck.

He realized he actually knew very little about the diagnostician other than her professional credits. She liked to work alone— as she herself had admitted—and she'd sometimes run into trouble with the hospital administrators back in the States because of the bullheaded way she went about her work. But she got the job done. And since she avoided being involved in treatment meetings, she circumvented some of the bureaucracy hospitals—even Hope Hospital—were known for.

"Did your mum die at Christmas?"

His daughter's young voice asking such hard questions caused a prickling sensation behind his eyes. One he quickly forced back. He knew he shouldn't be standing here eavesdropping on their conversation, but since they so rarely talked about Hope, he couldn't bring himself to interrupt them.

"She didn't *die* at Christmas. I don't know when she died, actually. I just know she did."

"That's sad. What about your daddy? Is he in heaven too?"

He wasn't sure why Madison hadn't cut off this topic before it got this far, but she'd offered up the information about her mother without his daughter asking about it.

"I never knew my father, so I don't know if he's in heaven or not."

*Hell.*

"How did Santa find you to give you your presents, then?"

That was his cue to put a stop to the prying. He knocked on the door a little louder than necessary and went on in to find the pair of them on Ivy's bed. There was no sign of giggling this time, though.

Madison was seated at the foot, across from his daughter, her legs drawn up and tucked beneath her thighs, her shoes on the floor beneath the bed. It was an incredibly casual and intimate scene. He could picture Hope doing exactly the same thing.

Only this wasn't Hope and he would do well to remember that. Madison was a temporary fixture in his daughter's life. He needed to remember that too, and he needed to find a way to let Ivy know she would be leaving eventually.

But that could wait until later. When she was better.

"Santa knows where everyone is." By bringing the conversation back around, and forcing a lightness to his voice that he did not feel, he hoped that Madison would think he'd just come in on the tail end of their conversation. When she tilted her head to glance up at him, her eyes said she knew exactly what he'd heard. But she didn't seem angry that he'd been standing there. If anything, she seemed relieved.

"Hi, Daddy!"

"Hi, sweetheart." He came in the rest of the way and gave his daughter a kiss on the head, frowning slightly. Did her brown hair seem a little less lustrous than it used to? Or was that his crazy thoughts leading him down dark paths again?

The little notebook Madison seemed to like so well was half-tucked under her left thigh. Writing down ideas? Or measuring Ivy's reflexes and drawing an arrow that was slowly angling down and gaining speed?

He was killing himself here. Ivy seemed in fairly good spirits, even after talking about her mother being in heaven. Of course she was too young to really remember Hope, even though photos of her peppered his apartment and office as a reminder.

The pack of cards was back in its box. Theo frowned. "Aren't we playing cards?"

"Sorry," Madison said. "I wasn't sure when you were going to be free, so we played without you, and we just finished up, actually."

"And I won, Daddy!"

"You did?" He smiled a question at the diagnostician he hoped she could decipher.

"She did very well." Madison gave a slight nod of her head. "Naomi was in earlier to do her therapy. Tomorrow good old Doodle will be coming in."

The therapy dog. Ivy seemed enamored with the dog already. Just like she was enamored with Madison. The thing was, neither of them would be sticking around in her life, and Theo wasn't sure it was a good idea for his daughter to get attached to either of them. He didn't want another scenario where something that was a constant in her life was suddenly snatched away.

Maybe it was time for him to set a few

boundaries, much as he disliked doing so. "Can I speak to you outside for a moment?"

Madison frowned, but she uncurled her legs and stood, tucking her notebook into her pocket. His eyes lingered on the book. His curiosity about it was getting out of hand. As were a lot of other things.

Like noticing how her bare feet were pink from being tucked underneath her, with the little toe on her right foot having a small crook to it. And nail polish. Glittery silver that seemed so out of character compared to the short plain nails on her hands. As if realizing she'd revealed something she preferred no one see, she hurriedly shoved her feet back into her low-heeled black pumps and tweaked a strand of Ivy's hair before preceding him out of the room and heading for the waiting area. He half expected her to go to his office, but maybe it was just as well that he address this in a public setting. Especially after being caught staring at her toes.

She dropped into one of the plush leather chairs, a luxury, yes, but Theo figured if parents were going to have to sit for hours and wait for potentially devastating news, they deserved something other than hard plastic. The leather could still be disinfected, with nooks and crannies kept to a minimum, while still being comfortable with supportive cushioning on the back. He moved to sit in the one across from her, leaning to prop his elbows on his knees.

Fortunately, no one else was there at the moment, since the bulk of the procedures would have been done earlier in the day. Most of the family suites had two rooms, one with a pull-out couch where parents could sleep near their children. There was also a playroom down the hallway with educational toys and movies for parents who had other children with them.

But none of that was important right now, and Madison was sitting with tightly clasped hands, waiting for him to get on with whatever he wanted to say to her.

"She's doing okay?"

"Yes. She hasn't gotten any worse over the last couple of days, so that's a good thing."

Yes, it was. At least the arrow he'd pictured taking a plunge wasn't a reality. But that wasn't why he'd asked to speak with her.

He decided to start with what he'd heard of their conversation. "I hope Ivy didn't ask a lot of personal questions in there. If so, I apologize. She doesn't always understand the concept of boundaries."

"About my parents? No, it's okay. And after she'd shared about her mom, I thought it might help her to not feel like she was the only child in the world who'd lost someone. I'm sorry if you'd rather I hadn't said anything."

"No, not at all." And he hadn't even thought about that being her reason for sharing. His reasons for asking her to come out here now seemed petty and mean. The woman was trying to figure out what was wrong with his daughter, for God's sake, and he wanted her to back off? Yes, Ivy was getting attached, but did he really want her growing up in a world that didn't form connections? Would he have rather never loved her mother?

Madison didn't know when her mother had died, or even who her father was. How was that for not having a good foundation?

The words came out before he was aware they'd formed. "I'm sorry about your mother."

"Thank you. But I didn't grow up with her. At least, not my whole life."

"You were adopted." Talk about prying questions.

"No, I wasn't that lucky." She sat there for

a few seconds and then continued. "My mom overdosed on Christmas Eve when I was ten. I didn't realize it until I got up the next morning and there were no presents under the tree. We were poor, but there was normally a gift or two."

Damn. "You said you didn't know when she died."

"That overdose wasn't fatal, but it was the last one I experienced with her. I found her on the floor in the kitchen. There was a needle on the counter and a roll of wrapping paper where she'd evidently been trying to wrap a Christmas gift for me. It was a bracelet-making kit." She shrugged. "I don't know what happened to that. It didn't come with me."

"To the hospital?"

"No. I was put in foster care. I remember sitting in a police car for a long time while they tried to find a place for me—not an easy task on a holiday, when gifts had already been purchased. The female officer was really nice, though. She bought me a fast-food meal and hugged me as I cried and asked a million times about my mom.

"My mom lived. That time. And I saw her periodically for about a year as I went from one set of foster parents to another, until it was finally a group home for me." She smiled. "Believe it or not, I was a little difficult to deal with as a child. I bet if you ask anyone at my other hospital, they'll tell you I still am."

She may have been trying to make light of a difficult situation, but it didn't work. "I have a feeling it made you tenacious—not difficult."

"A nice way of saying the same thing." Her smile faded. "Anyway, Christmas doesn't hold the best memories for that reason. I actually have the perfect career imaginable for someone like me, since most doctors have to work at least some Christmases. I simply choose to work them all."

Christmas was hard for him too, but he did the opposite because of Ivy. He would have liked to work his way through that particular holiday as well, but he wanted his daughter to have good memories, even if he didn't. "I understand that completely. My late wife died at Christmastime."

"Ivy said you were sad this time of year."

"My daughter is far too wise for her years."

"Children like us don't have a choice." She stopped suddenly. "I didn't mean that the way it sounded. You're a great dad. Ivy is very lucky."

Right now it didn't feel like either of those things was true. As much as he tried to make time for his daughter, he still worked long hours. His housekeeper had stepped in to help time and time again. And as far as being lucky, looking at Ivy and her condition, it didn't feel like she was very lucky.

"I can't be with her as much as I'd like to, but Judy helps fill in some of those gaps."

Her eyes widened slightly. "Judy?"

"Sorry. She's our housekeeper. She also plays nanny more often than I would like."

"Is she the older lady who has been in to visit? I assumed she was Ivy's grandmother."

That was another way Madison and Ivy were connected. Neither of them had grandparents. Well, he assumed Madison didn't since she'd been in foster care and had only mentioned visits from her mother and not grandparents. "No, my folks passed away when I was in medical school, and Hope's mom has Alzheimer's and is in a care home."

"I'm sorry." She hesitated. "You mentioned having a housekeeper. I never associated that with having someone to watch Ivy while you work."

"It's not an ideal situation, and I will be the first to admit it. I don't have time to cook and clean like some fathers do."

"I wasn't criticizing you. I just…" She let her voice trail off.

She sounded almost apologetic, although he had no idea what she had to be sorry for.

"I didn't take it as criticism." His elbows were still planted on his knees, but somehow he had leaned in, the long curtain of Madison's hair close enough to touch. And hell if he didn't want to.

To keep from acting on that impulse, he twined his fingers together and used the resulting fist to rest his chin on.

He'd brought her here to ask her to be careful of how attached she was letting Ivy get, and here he was thinking about toying with strands of that silky hair.

"Can I ask you something?"

"Of course." Even as he gave her permission, something in him tensed up.

"It's personal. And hard."

The tension turned into rigid muscles and a frozen brain. "What is it?"

"Your wife's name was Hope?"

Damn, the last thing he wanted to talk to her about was his late wife. "Yes."

"Is there any way I can get a copy of Hope's medical records? And yours?"

"I'm sorry?"

"That came out badly. I want to see if there's anything in there I can spot. Maybe a genetic component that's been overlooked."

She thought he or Hope had passed something to Ivy that was making her sick? "Didn't they do that when they were looking for muscular dystrophy?"

"Yes, but there are other things. How did your wife die?"

"She was hit by a car while out walking Ivy." His voice was a little harsher than he'd meant it to be, but she was right. These were personal questions.

Her chin went up a bit. And her words about being a difficult child came back to him. He had a feeling she wasn't going to back down until she got whatever it was she was after.

"Did you notice any unsteadiness in her before it happened? Any changes in her behavior?"

Had there been? He cast around for the last time he'd seen his wife. It had been that morning when he'd left for work. They'd made love the night before, and she'd made him breakfast before he'd left the house the next morning. No unsteadiness. Just a loving woman who had been far too patient about his long hours.

"No. She was perfect. In every way."

Madison didn't move for a second. Then she reached a hand toward him. "I'm sorry, Theo. Really I am."

He allowed himself to capture her fingers, while he tried to process his thoughts. "What do you expect to find in her records? In mine?"

"It's not what I expect to find. I've just hit a brick wall time and time again with the test results. I thought maybe I could look at each of you separately and see if there's anything I could use as a springboard." Without unlinking their hands, she moved to the chair next to his and turned to face him. "Is there any possibility Hope could have had Huntington's?"

A degenerative brain disease, it showed itself in uncoordinated muscle movements, followed by cognitive decline. It was inherited and deadly, passed from mother to daughter. If Ivy had that…

Well, he didn't want to think of the ramifications. Any hope he'd had of a cure would go out the window. And how would he know if Hope had had it, really? Could she have fallen in front of that car rather than the other way around? The driver had been arrested and convicted, but what if there had been something insidious he'd missed?

How far would Madison be willing to go to follow her hunches? How far would he let her go? All thoughts of Doodle and attachments disappeared.

"Look at her records. Look at mine. But I don't want to exhume Hope's body."

Madison squeezed his fingers. "I don't either. I'd just like to chase this rabbit for a little while." She paused. "But only as long as I think it's useful. I'm not at the point of throwing spaghetti against a wall and seeing what sticks."

"And if I'm ready to do just that?" Would he actually allow them to dig up her body? He wasn't sure.

"Do you really want Ivy to go through a battery of unnecessary tests?"

No. He didn't. She'd already gone through her share and more. "I'll have Hope's records pulled. But I'd like to go through them with you."

"Of course." Her eyes searched his. "And yours?"

"Yes. I'll make sure you have those as well." He had nothing to hide. At least nothing in his medical history. As for his current history... Oh, yes. He had things he would rather Madison not know about. Like the way her hand in his felt reassuring. And unnerving. And anything except platonic.

"Do you really think it could be Huntington's?"

"No, but I'd rather not leave any stone unturned. Like multiple sclerosis, Huntington's is normally found in adults, but it can appear in young children on rare occasions. I don't see any mental decline in Ivy, though. Quite the contrary. That little girl is a card shark. She bats those big innocent eyelashes at you, all the while waiting for an opportunity to do a smack down."

"A smack down?"

"You know."

"No, I really don't." But it was a good confusion. Something that felt shared.

"It's an expression."

"I see." He paused, trying to get back on track, but not enough to let go of her hand. "So what other genetic conditions could it be?"

"I need to do some research. Huntington's

was the only thing that came to mind, but her wobbliness made me think of that. Which led me to think of genes. The dystrophies are normally genetic, but the muscle biopsy ruled that out. But there are lots of other possibilities."

"Lots is not a word I want to hear."

"I'm not looking at it like that. There are lots of possibilities, yes, but all it takes is one. And that one is what I'm eying at the moment. I just ruled out polymyositis. She's developed foot drop in her right ankle, which is what made me think of it, but her torso and neck flexion seem normal."

An inflammation of muscle tissue, polymyositis could affect the heart and/or the lungs, so he was glad she'd ruled that out. Although a Huntington's diagnosis would be as bad, if not worse.

She jiggled his hand, and touched her shoulder to his, bringing his mind back to her. "Hey, I'm just trying to be thorough. We can't help her until we know what it is. A steroid for a few days might not be a bad idea, though."

She turned her head to look at something and the scent of her shampoo floated toward him, along with some lighter, more feminine fragrance.

He swallowed. He'd been doing okay. Until now.

She was still talking but the words began to flow together into a long incoherent string of sound as his mind zoomed in on the warmth of her fingers in his, her grip tightening and relaxing as she worked through another thought. Within seconds, the sensation eclipsed the rational side of his brain, leaving it open to attack from other areas. And attack they did.

The pleasure centers went on the prowl, cruising along the aisles of awareness. An awareness that had been simmering in the background ever since they'd met.

"...we could also try activating some of those neural receptors and see what happens..."

His fingers tightened on hers. She was already activating some of those neural receptors and it was pretty obvious—to him—what was happening.

Her head tilted as she studied his face. "Theo? Are you okay?"

This was the moment of truth. Admit it, or pretend there was nothing wrong. Only she'd already noticed something wasn't right. If he tried to lie, he could end up making things a hundred times worse.

Was he crazy? How could they be any worse than they already were?

"Theo?"

"Actually, I'm struggling with something." Maybe it was the revelations about her mom that cast Madison in a different light—the reasons for the slight standoffishness he'd noticed from time to time suddenly making sense. Or maybe it was the stress of dealing with Ivy's illness that had his senses out of whack. But he found himself wanting to do something crazy and impulsive, something he hadn't analyzed from every angle before acting on it.

"With what?"

"The way your thoughts dart from one thing to the other so fast that I can barely keep up."

"I—I'm sorry."

"Don't be. I like it. But it also drives me… insane. In ways I should be able to control." Letting go of her hand, he curled his fingers around the nape of her neck, his thumb sliding just beneath her jaw to where he knew her pulse beat. He let his fingers trail down the side of her throat, along skin that was incredibly soft. "But right now I don't want to control it. And that's the struggle. So... I need you to tell me to back off."

She moistened her lips and started to say something, then stopped. Her eyes met his. "I don't think I can."

Something inside him leaped to attention and he lowered his voice, aware that they were still completely alone. "You *can't* tell me to back off, or you don't want to?" He leaned forward, employing light pressure to bring her nearer until their lips were a mere centimeter away.

"I don't want to tell you...want you to..." Her hand went to his shoulder, fingers pressing through the thin fabric of his button-down shirt. Warmth bloomed and traveled. And then, with a feeling of déjà vu, her mouth touched his.

Senses that had been dormant for years erupted in a huge array of lights that rendered him blind for several seconds.

When he could see again, he was kissing her back and Theo knew at that moment he was in big trouble. He should stop this before it went any further, but his limbs wouldn't cooperate. Neither would his mouth.

So there was nothing else to do but sit back and enjoy the ride. Because any time now Madison was sure to realize what a mistake this was and call a screeching halt to it.

All of it.

And when that happened, Theo had no idea what he was going to do.

# CHAPTER FIVE

MADISON'S BODY WAS turned at a weird angle, but she didn't care. She would have stayed there until her muscle strength totally deserted her. In fact, she dragged herself closer, even as something about that last thought tugged at her.

No. She didn't want to think. She wanted to feel. How long had it been since she'd been in someone's embrace?

Far too long.

The men who found her aloofness attractive at first were soon disillusioned when that didn't magically shift into something softer. She wasn't capable of softness. To be soft was to be vulnerable, and to be vulnerable was to be hurt.

Except her softer side showed through around one little girl.

And now around that little girl's father.

His hands came up and cupped her face and a sound rumbled up in his chest, a half sigh, half groan that had her reacting in ways that were foreign to her. She didn't normally stick around long enough to form attachments. But Madison suddenly wanted to set this man's world on fire, and she had no idea why. Her tongue slid forward, catching her first real taste of his mouth.

*Heaven, pure heaven.* Just like she knew he'd taste.

But how?

Her muscles weakened further, sending her thoughts skittering back to another place. A place she didn't want to be. Her hand slipped off his shoulder as a pressure grew behind her eyelids.

Muscle weakness.

Wheelchairs.

Possible…

*Ivy!*

She dragged her mouth from his in an instant as reality swamped her. What was she doing? This was her patient's father.

No. Ivy wasn't solely her patient.

Did that matter? She might have a string of doctors as long as her arm, but Madison was definitely on that list.

"Sorry, Theo. I'm sorry." She tried to suck down a few deep breaths to ward off the light-headedness that was doing wonky things to her thought processes.

He stared at her for a second, then dragged the back of his hand across his mouth. Trying to wipe away her touch?

Her heart slammed against her ribs in protest, even as he shook his head.

"I'm the one who should be apologizing. God, Maddy, I have no idea where that came from."

She swallowed hard. No one called her Maddy. No one. Not since the last time she'd seen her mom. It was part of the problem she'd had in foster care, lashing out anytime someone had tried to shorten her name to something more familiar.

She hadn't wanted familiar. She'd wanted distance. After her prom disaster that need had grown.

But this time?

Trying not to acknowledge the little thrill that went through her at hearing him call her that—and trying to reject the kernel of an idea that Theo's kiss had sparked an indefinable change between them—she sat back in her seat. "It was me. Or maybe the struggle to find an answer to Ivy's condition. We're both tired. Stressed. And definitely not ourselves."

At least, Madison wasn't herself. Whether Theo was acting out of character or not was for him to decide.

"No, not ourselves." He glanced around. "That was unprofessional, especially since I wanted to mention an item of concern."

"Besides the kiss?"

He gave a visible grimace. "Yes. Ivy has suffered one terrible loss in her life. I wonder whether allowing her to get too attached…" There was a huge pause in which he seemed to be searching for something.

Oh, God. He thought Ivy was getting too attached to her? Was he going to ask her to back off the case? And if he did? As Ivy's father, he certainly had the right to do whatever he wanted.

He finally continued his thought. "Whether getting too attached to Doodle—is that his name?—is a good idea. What happens when he no longer comes back to visit her."

Theo might be genuinely worried about that, but his words made her sag into her seat in relief. She'd been so sure he was going to point that accusing finger at her. And he might be right, if he had. She had been spending a lot of time with the little girl. But then she spent a lot of time with all her patients. It was how she did her job.

"I was afraid you were going to say I was the problem. And I want to assure you that I do the same thing with each and every one of my patients. It's not that Ivy isn't special. Of course she is. It's just my process. I do whatever I have to do to come up with a diagnosis."

Even as she said the words, Theo flinched. Damn. She'd made it sound like she kissed all her patients' fathers.

"That's not what was behind that..." She couldn't even bring herself to say the word. What if that was why *he'd* kissed *her*? Because he was desperate and willing to do anything to help his daughter?

So what was her excuse?

Just what she'd told him. She was stressed at not being able to come up with an answer for him. Strong emotions needed a pressure valve or they exploded. So had his kiss been the valve? Or the explosion?

Something she didn't want to look at.

*But someday, Madison, you're going to have to. Because unless you actually remove*

*yourself from Ivy's case—ha!—emotions are*
*bound to get out of hand again, eventually.*

Not a good thing. She needed to figure out
how to contain them enough to avoid getting
into another situation like this one.

"That's good to know. It was a simple mis-
step on both of our parts. You are an attractive woman who is smart and funny and who
my child seems to enjoy being around. And
I let things spiral out of control." He paused
a beat or two. "I think you hit the nail on
the head earlier. There are a lot of unknowns
right now. That kiss was one of those unknowns. Hopefully now that we're aware
of the possibility, we won't let ourselves be
drawn into situations where one—or both—
of us might react without thinking of the consequences."

"Consequences?"

"What it might mean for Ivy if someone
thinks you're getting preferential treatment."

She forced a laugh. "Exactly what kind of
preferential treatment would that be? Getting
to kiss the mighty Theo Hawkwood?"

The comment might contain a hint of
snark, but it was only to cover up how shaken
she still was. And how being this close to
him was still working on her nerve centers.

Which wanted to kiss him all over again, damn them.

"How about if someone saw us and thinks you're playing some kind of angle?"

Her soul froze. What if someone actually did think she was trying to work her way up some corporate ladder—or angling for an invitation to stay in Cambridge and continue to work at Hope Hospital? It happened all the time, didn't it? What if Theo himself thought she was doing that? Could that be why he'd mentioned it?

The frozen spot inside her grew. Madison had worked hard her entire life. She'd never had anything handed to her. And certainly not because she'd tried to manipulate someone into it. "I—I would never—"

"I know you wouldn't, Maddy. I wasn't trying to say that. People could just as easily think I'm abusing my position and sexually harassing you."

"Which I would *assure* them you weren't." The ice was turning into a block that encased her heart. The same one that had surrounded it when her first set of foster parents had asked to have her transferred elsewhere. She'd soon figured out that nothing in her life was permanent. So why bother trying. Thank heavens she'd finally channeled all that anger and despair into her studies once she'd hit college and medical school. Her stubborn unwillingness to bend or give in had served her in good stead. And as a diagnostician, she had taken what had seemed like a personality defect and turned it into an asset.

Theo held his hands up. "Okay. Let's both acknowledge our part in this fiasco and work to fix it."

"Agreed."

"We can start by going out on the town. I have a day off coming up a week from Thursday on Christmas Eve and a couple of half-days before that."

"Going out on the town...together?"

"Yes."

Her brows shot up. "Are you crazy? Or just plain nuts?" That was a little over a week away. Not nearly enough time to section off the memory of what had just happened into a different part of her brain.

He grinned. "It would seem both. But maybe if we get away from the hospital for a couple of hours and do things that don't revolve around patients or tests or the millions of other things we do on a daily basis, we could unwind in ways that are a bit safer."

"Safer. What about Ivy?"

"As long as she's having a good day, I don't see how it can hurt anything. She doesn't require twenty-four-seven nursing care."

Not yet. But if Madison couldn't figure out what was wrong with her, it could very well come to that. She pushed that thought away. "I don't know."

"I'm not trying to pressure you, but I think it would do us both some good, and I know for a fact that you've spent almost all of your free time in Ivy's room."

That was true. What if Theo was right, and that kiss had been caused by being pulled one way and then the other until she'd gone past the breaking point? It would be stupid to turn him down in that case, wouldn't it?

"Well, as long as Ivy is doing okay, I guess it wouldn't hurt."

He pulled out his wallet. "In fact, I happen to have an extra ticket to a carol service at King's College, compliments of the parents of a patient, if you're interested." Producing a ticket, he held it out to her.

"A carol service? As in Christmas carols?" A tense note entered her voice, but she wasn't sure how to get rid of it.

"You've never heard of Carols from King's?"

"Yes, but I thought that was pre-recorded earlier in the month."

He nodded. "The actual program is, but the college also holds a carol service on Christmas Eve at three o'clock."

She wrinkled her nose. "I'm not much of a Christmas person, for the reasons I explained earlier. I tolerate the season, but would rather not attend anything dedicated to it."

"It's a church service. Santa Claus doesn't even make an appearance." He took her palm and placed the ticket in it. "It's extra. I have my own ticket. So keep it in case you change your mind."

Her fingers closed around it, trying to ignore the warmth from his body that permeated the piece of card. "You won't be offended if I decide not to go? Maybe someone else can use the ticket."

"No, I normally go by myself. The extra ticket has gone to waste for the last four years."

Because he'd taken his wife before that? That made her heart ache, and she couldn't bring herself to refuse to keep it. How many of those extra tickets had he tossed in the garbage?

"Thank you." She took out her notebook

and slid the ticket inside it before replacing it in her pocket.

Just then the elevator doors opened and Marco Ricci emerged. He started to turn left then stopped and glanced their way. He gave a half-wave. "I was just getting ready to head to your office," he called to Theo.

"Is the surgery docket full again?"

"What?" Then, as if he realized what Theo was asking, he headed over toward them, reaching out to shake his hand. "No, today we have it all under control."

He glanced at Madison. "By the way, I heard you lent a hand in the surgical suite the other day. Thank you."

"I did more observing than anything, but you're welcome."

He smiled again. "Actually, it's good that you're both here. Alice and I are planning a private little soirée on Saturday evening." He cleared his throat. "Actually, we're getting married. We're going for a big celebration in Italy later, but neither one of us wants to wait. And...we need two witnesses. We would be honored if you would do that for us, if you can. You've come to mean a lot to Alice in the time you've been here, Madison, so she really wants you to be there. She was going to come and ask you directly, but she's been swamped with work and with plans for the baby."

Alice was pregnant and positively glowing with health and happiness.

Looking at Theo, she suddenly didn't care if he agreed to do it or not. If anyone deserved to be happy, it was Alice and Marco. "I'd love to. What time?"

"Six in the evening. Will that do?"

"Yes. Absolutely."

Marco stuffed his hands in his pockets. "And you, Theo. Are you game?"

"I would be honored. Just let me know where."

"It'll be at Hotel Cambridge du Monde."

Theo gave a quiet whistle. "Flying high nowadays, are we?"

"In more ways than one." He clapped Theo on the shoulder. "I can hardly believe my good fortune. Alice and our baby. What more could a man want?"

"What more indeed." There was a wistfulness to Theo's voice that made sharp tears prick behind Madison's eyelids. Was he thinking about his late wife and all he'd lost?

"It's going to be a very small ceremony, but Alice wants her colors to be green or red, since she'll have red roses and green ivy in her bouquet. So, if you can scrounge up one of those two colors, that would be great. If not, just come as you are."

Madison racked her brain, but she hadn't brought a dress at all, much less a green or red one. Which meant she'd have to go out and buy something in town. Instead of spending a whole day with Theo, and feeling like she needed to go to that carol service with him, maybe they could just roll the wedding and a quick shopping trip into one joint venture. Hopefully that was one of his half-days off.

It would help keep her mind focused on a task rather than the man she was with. The timing was perfect. And Theo would know the town much better than she did. "Is it formal?"

"Not black-tie formal, but we're doing dresses and suits."

So not long dresses but something short. And a fascinator? Did they wear those to less formal events? She would wait and ask Alice the next time she saw her. Or Naomi. Wow, she just realized that people were falling in love and getting married all around her. She was on the outside, looking in.

Just like always.

The way she liked it.

"I'm really happy for you both," she said. She hadn't gotten up from her seat like Theo had because her legs were currently shaky and she felt a little out of sorts after everything that had happened.

"Thanks, we're quite over the moon ourselves." Marco glanced at the elevator, which had long since traveled to some other floor. "Well, I've got a surgery to scrub for. I just wanted to come up and ask you in person rather than ring you. Alice will be thrilled you've both agreed to come. If you have any questions, call her. She's the boss."

They said their goodbyes and then Marco was gone, off to his next stop in a full and happy life.

"I have nothing to wear to a wedding. Any chance we can skip Thursday and shop for something before the ceremony? I can just change at the hotel before that. Unless you can't get the time off."

"It won't be a problem. I'll get a tie to match your dress while we're at it. It wouldn't do to have Alice be cross with me. Because that would make Marco cross and probably everyone else at the venue."

So much for them each going their separate ways in town. It seemed that they were stuck shopping together. But since they had a destination afterwards, their day would be pretty much programmed down to the last second. Which left no time for anything else to happen.

Like kissing.

Or worse.

Because when they'd been kissing, she'd definitely wanted it to lead to something worse. Thank God they'd come to their senses before Marco had come up here. Because that would have been a disaster in the making.

And with Ivy's life hanging in the balance, that was something neither she nor Theo could afford.

Thursday evening, Theo had gathered his and Hope's medical records and spread them out on his desk for Maddy to see. She pored over them page by page, her green eyes slowly perusing charts and tests, down to the smallest details such as blood types. "Your mom had diabetes. No sign of anything in you, though."

"No. She had type one. I don't."

And diabetes certainly wouldn't be behind whatever was happening with Ivy. It was a lost cause. She'd already been through Hope's records and found nothing. No hint of a genetic anomaly, although it still couldn't be ruled out. Theo could have told her that, but he understood why Maddy wanted to see it for herself. No muscle-wasting diseases in either of their family histories that they knew of. And definitely no Huntington's disease.

Having Hope's records on his desk hurt, but not in the sharp, unfathomable way it once had. It was more of a wistful longing for his daughter to have known her mother. He'd loved Hope, there was no doubt about it. But she was gone. It had taken him a long time to accept the fact that she wasn't going to walk into the room one day and wrap her arms around his neck the way she once had.

Was he okay with that?

He'd accepted it, if that counted. He would always carry a part of her with him. Ivy was the greatest gift she could have given him. And he would always be grateful for what they'd had. His biggest regret was not having been a better husband to her. He had the same regret with his daughter, although he had learned his lesson and made a conscious effort to spend more time with Ivy. Not as much as he'd like, but her illness had been a wake-up call to focus on the truly important things in life.

With fewer distractions.

Like the beautiful distraction sitting on the other side of the desk?

Yes, he had been distracted ever since she'd set foot in his hospital. That seemed to be growing worse by the day. He was hoping that going shopping together would fix the shock of awareness that happened every time he ran across her in unexpected places. Like sleeping in his daughter's room.

Which reminded him. "Are you spending the night in Ivy's room?

She blinked, her teeth coming down on her lip. "Not every night, no. Sometimes if I'm working on a case late at night, I stop in to check on her, and I'm too tired to go home. I end up falling asleep in the chair next to her bed."

He knew. He'd come into Ivy's room and caught her curled in a ball in that chair beside his daughter's bed, her hair flowing down the dark fabric. As hard as he'd tried not to stand there and watch the pair of them, he'd been held in the grip of some strange emotion. It was like seeing Hope and Ivy together again. Only Madison didn't look like his wife. She wasn't Ivy's mother.

And right now she sounded a little defensive. He hadn't meant it as an accusation. Time to put her mind at ease, even if he couldn't do the same for his own.

"I wasn't criticizing. I've just been sleeping on the pull-out couch in the next room and have tried not to wake either of you. That chair can't be comfortable. I was just going to offer the couch in my office on the nights you work late."

"I had no idea you were going in and sleeping there—I'm sorry for intruding."

"You weren't. I'm normally out of there early in the morning. But I didn't want you to think she was alone at night, if that was part of the reason you were staying there."

"I know. And she has nurses check in on her regularly. It's just quieter there than in the staff lounge, and the chairs in the rooms aren't that uncomfortable."

"For sleeping? Yes, they are. Just stretch out on the couch in my office. It is quiet, and I promise I won't disturb you." He grinned. "You can hang a sign on the door if you want."

"Thank you. I may take you up on it. There are days I could fall asleep anywhere."

"Please do. Like I said, since we moved Ivy into the room, I've been sleeping on the couch in there, so the office is unoccupied at night."

And seeing her dozing in that chair, looking so soft and vulnerable, also did a number on him. Maybe the subtle hint would move her out of reach. Or at least out of his sight. Several times he'd been tempted to offer the guest couch in the adjoining room. But Ivy was his daughter, and his place was there with her, not in his office.

"Thank you again. That sounds like a great idea." She turned her head to the right. "And maybe I can get rid of this crick in my neck."

A quick stab of guilt went through him, even though he knew she hadn't meant it that way.

"I'm sorry about that."

"Don't be. It was my choice to sleep there." She straightened a row of papers on his desk. "I, um, didn't realize you'd been coming in at night. The couch is never unfolded in the morning. I hope I wasn't snoring or anything when you walked by."

"I try to fold everything back up before

I leave. As for snoring, you hardly make a peep. Just a tiny snuffle every once in a while."

Which he found adorable and charming.

"A snuffle? Ugh. Don't tell me that." She paused. "You must not sleep for eight hours at a shot, or I would have seen you at some point."

"No, I rarely do. My body doesn't need more than six hours at any given time."

Plus the fact that he hadn't wanted to come face to face with Madison in the morning with sleepy eyes and mussed hair. So he set his watch for a time he knew she'd be still asleep. Another reason to offer her the couch in his office. Those restless nights were beginning to tell on him.

As if on cue, she yawned. He glanced at his watch and saw it was almost ten o'clock. "Why don't we call it a night? We can leave everything here, if you still need to look at them some more."

"I think I've seen everything I need to see." She hesitated again and then started gathering pages together into stacks. "Are you sleeping in Ivy's room tonight?"

"I am. I was just waiting to finish up here. So why don't you take my couch, like we talked about?" He helped her finish straightening and showed her into the adjoining sitting room, which had the same cozy furniture as the rest of the hospital. "There are sheets and blankets and a pillow in the closet. Are you on call in the morning?"

"Yes. At six."

Which made him feel bad about keeping her up so late, even though this had been her idea. "It's settled, then."

"Are you sure?"

"Absolutely." It was the best solution for everyone. He could sleep in peace knowing she was comfortable. And he wouldn't be kept awake thinking about her being in the next room, with that quiet snuffling to remind him of that fact every couple of minutes. Although he would miss knowing she was close by. More than he cared to admit.

"Okay, then, I appreciate it."

"You can just close the door to the suite and have complete privacy. There's a bathroom with a shower in there as well." Theo stacked the two medical folders on the corner of his desk. "I'll return these tomorrow."

"Sounds good." She suppressed yet another yawn, and he decided that was his cue to leave. "You can text or call me if you need anything or if you have a question."

With that he gathered his keys and wallet and headed for the door. "See you sometime tomorrow."

"Thank you again."

She waited until he had shut the door before stretching her aching muscles. Leaning over that desk, even from a seated position, had caused her shoulders and neck to cramp. But, more than that, she was frustrated that she hadn't found the answers she'd been looking for. No hint or clue as to what could be behind Ivy's condition. Swiveling her torso from side to side in an effort to loosen things up, she prowled around Theo's office, peering curiously at various medical degrees and awards he'd earned over the years—things she hadn't noticed since she hadn't been in his office very many times.

Moving to get a closer look at a commendation letter on the wall about Hope Hospital, a frame on his desk caught her attention. When she'd been studying their medical charts the frame's back had been to her, so she hadn't known what was in it. She'd assumed it was a snapshot of Ivy. It wasn't.

Theo and a woman with a baby were in it. Theo was younger than the man she knew now, and there was no evidence of the frown lines he wore today. She picked up the picture to study it. The woman's peaches-and-cream complexion glowed with happiness as she cradled a baby. It had to be Ivy and her mother. The woman was beautiful, her long blonde hair shimmering with life and health.

She glanced at the wall again, something she'd seen earlier kicking to the forefront of her mind. There. Frame in hand, she moved past the far side of his desk toward the corner of the room. Hope Elizabeth Mueller was listed as having earned her Bachelor of Medicine and Bachelor of Surgery degrees—the equivalent of medical doctor degrees in the States. That had to be Ivy's mom. So she'd graduated from medical school before she and Theo married. And he'd named the hospital after her. She held the picture up and looked at it and the medical certificate together, trying to picture what Theo's and her life must have been like together.

Happy. That's what it had been.

How could anyone get over the once-in-a-lifetime love they must have shared?

A sudden sound behind her caused her fingers to open. The picture crashed to the floor with a sickening sound of broken glass.

She whirled around, already knowing she'd been caught red-handed, her snooping ending in catastrophe.

Theo stood in the doorway, his head cocked to the side as his gaze went to the desk and then to her. Then he frowned.

"Oh, God, Theo. I am so sorry. I saw the picture and was just looking at it and —"

"It's okay, Maddy. It was bound to break at some point."

Madison swallowed. What was bound to break? The frame? Or his heart?

"I had no business looking through your things." She squatted down to hurriedly gather broken pieces of glass, shuddering when she saw a white line down the photo where a shard had slid along the smooth surface. A hard knot formed in her stomach. What had she been thinking?

That she wouldn't have minded being the woman in the idyllic photo standing next to Theo, their baby cradled between them?

No, she hadn't been thinking that at all.

Theo moved to the other side of the desk to help her. "Don't worry about it." He glanced at the picture and carefully picked up some of the larger bits of glass.

She held out the photo. "Do you still have the file, so I can replace this?"

"I do somewhere, but I'll take care of it." He dumped a pile of glass on top of his desk and then turned the frame around to get the back off it.

He slid the picture free and shook it to remove any debris. There was writing on the other side of it. "To my love. A reminder to always come home to us at the end of the day."

She gulped, her vision blurring. It took several blinks to clear it. When she did, she realized Theo had spotted the words as well, a muscle in his jaw working as he stared at them. Then he turned it over and placed it flat on his desk. "I came in to get my shaving kit. Sorry. I thought you'd already gone to bed."

Obviously, she'd been rummaging through his things instead. No, she hadn't. The picture had simply caught her eye. He wouldn't have offered to let her use his office if he was embarrassed or ashamed of anything in here. Or if he didn't want her to see this picture.

But he certainly hadn't expected her to smash it to smithereens.

"That picture has been in the frame ever since she gave it to me. I never saw what was on the back of it."

He'd never looked on the other side of it?

*Don't cry, Madison.*

"I am so sorry."

"Don't be." He climbed to his feet and held out his hand. "I'll get the rest of it tomorrow."

She let him help her up and looked down at the photo. "She loved you very much."

"Yes." He didn't say anything for a long minute. "She died a week after this picture was taken. Just before Christmas. It was still wrapped and under the tree."

An image of a devastated Theo sitting under that tree and opening those presents by himself sent a stab of pain that was as sharp as any piece of glass twisting through her. "What happened?"

"Drunk driver. I was working. Just like I always was." He walked around to the front of his desk, leaving her to follow him. "We'd planned to share this office once the hospital was up and running. She never got a chance to do that, though. She gave up everything to sit at home and wait for me."

Madison frowned. "I'm sure she didn't

think of it like that. She looks very happy in that picture."

He picked it up and studied it. "Does she? I can't tell anymore. I can't even really picture her without the use of a photograph. I keep them up for Ivy's sake."

But not for his own? Did it hurt to see her face staring at him day after day? He'd changed—his face maturing into hard, craggy lines of determination. Did he wonder what she would look like five years later? Or was she forever immortalized as young and beautiful? And hopeful?

Ivy talked about her father being sad. And Madison could see why.

"Let me replace the frame."

"I'll get one tomorrow. It's not a problem."

Maybe not for him. But it was for her. Her stupidity had evidently unleashed a dam of pain he'd had walled up inside him. He'd never even seen that inscription before? What a tragic situation. And now the daughter in that picture was sick, and possibly fighting for her life. And just like with the death of his wife, Theo probably felt helpless to change anything.

So that meant it was up to her. She *had* to find a reason for Ivy's weakness so they could take measures to reverse it, or at least stop its progression. And she would. If she had to work twenty-four hours a day and scour every medical journal known to man, she was going to figure this out. All that channeled stubbornness? This was what she'd been born to do.

And do it she would.

She went over and put her hand on Theo's arm and looked up into his eyes. "I'm going to find that answer for you, Theo, whether it's tomorrow or the next day. I'm going to do it. And it's going to be soon."

# CHAPTER SIX

MADISON STARED INTO the microscope and drew in a deep breath. Bacterial meningitis. It had taken all of five minutes to request the test be run and have a readout confirm her suspicions. She pushed back from the desk and headed out to the ICU department, where the child's worried mom was waiting for her to put in an appearance. Hopefully they'd caught it early enough for the boy to make a complete recovery.

She saw Alice in the hallway. She was in street clothes, so she obviously wasn't on duty today. Not that she'd expect her to be.

"What are you doing here? I thought you'd be getting ready for the wedding?"

"I'm on my way out now. I had a surgery to do."

Leave it to the dedicated surgeon to work until the very last second.

Like Theo used to do before Hope had died?

Ugh! She needed to stop thinking about that picture. But it had haunted her day and night. Two days later, it was still frameless. She'd been so busy working that she hadn't had time to buy a replacement frame. And knowing the picture was still lying on his desk, like an accusation, had kept her from using that couch a second time. Would Hope have considered it a betrayal that Theo had let her in to use his private office? That he'd kissed her?

Great. She was going to drive herself crazy at this rate.

Alice glanced at her face, maybe seeing something there she didn't like. "You and Theo are still planning to come this evening, aren't you?"

"Yes, of course. I have to go shopping for a dress in a little while but, yes."

"Okay, great. We'll see you there around six, then. Talk to you later."

They said their goodbyes and Madison continued on her way, entering her patient's room a few minutes later. Kyle Saunders was hooked up to a ventilator and the sight and sounds of the machines up by his head monitoring blood pressure and respiration had to be a heartbreaking sight for any parent.

"Any news at all?" Shirley Saunders, a single mom of two young boys, got up from her chair, her bloodshot eyes the only spot of color in an otherwise pale face.

"Yes. He has meningitis. We're going to start an IV antibiotic and some medicines that will hopefully keep the swelling in his brain to a minimum."

"Will he get better?"

She glanced at Kyle, whose still form was eerily silent. "Now that we have a definitive diagnosis, we're hopeful. We'll know soon after we start the antibiotics. Do we have your permission to treat him?"

"Of course. I'll sign anything. Just help my son."

Theo had said something very similar to her when she'd first arrived at the hospital. *Just help my daughter.*

"We'll do our best. We have a neurologist who is going to assess him as well and see where we stand."

Shirley clasped her hands in front of her. "Will he be like this forever?"

She assumed she meant in a coma.

"No." She could say that with all certainty,

because unless something unexpected happened, Kyle would either get better or he would die. She just didn't want to say that to his worried mom, unless it looked like it would come to that. "A nurse will be here in a few minutes to start the IV medication. And I'll be back to check on him before I leave today." She scribbled her cellphone number on a sheet of paper and gave it to her.

"I want you to call me if you have any questions once he begins treatment. The nurses are here to help as well. So don't be afraid to ask."

"I won't." A hand on her wrist stopped her for a second. "I can't thank you enough. I was warned it could be a while before they worked out what was wrong. It's only been a few hours."

"It's never as quick as we'd like it to be."

It certainly hadn't been in Ivy's case, despite the long hours she'd devoted to finding a cause. But she had a couple of new hunches she wanted to try out before she left to go shopping with Theo, whom she'd barely seen since she'd broken that frame.

She'd gotten up early and vacated the room that morning, hoping to avoid running into him. But first she'd finished cleaning up the glass, using a small hand vacuum she'd found in the same closet as the sheets and blankets. Then she'd folded all her linens and put them back where she'd found them. And his pillow...

She cringed, remembering how the fabric had trapped his scent from whenever he'd last used it, his musky aftershave melding with the essence of what made Theo unique. It had haunted her the entire night. Unable to resist, she'd hugged it close one last time, inhaling deeply before stuffing the thing into the closet and slamming the door shut.

Finally, she'd used her phone to snap a picture of the frame itself, hoping to run across something similar in their shopping travels this afternoon.

She'd been fairly successful at steering clear of Theo since then. But she couldn't avoid him forever. They had arranged to go shopping at three. She could only hope that she'd find a dress quickly and that she survived the wedding ceremony.

All she could do was take things one hour at a time and hope for the best.

Theo waited in his office for Maddy to finish her last case of the day. Picking up the picture, he turned it over again, just as he had for the last couple of days.

*A reminder to always come home to us.*

Which he hadn't always done. She'd been home alone many nights before Ivy had been born.

How had he not known that inscription was there? Because Hope had died before he'd opened the present. Otherwise she would have told him to look. He never had. Had never seen a reason to take it out of the safe place that had housed it for the last four and a half years.

Like the place that had housed his heart? The heart that hadn't ventured from that spot since the day Hope had died?

He flipped the photo back to the front and dragged a stack of folders and dropped them on top of it.

A knock sounded at the door, relieving him of his thoughts. He got up to answer it and found Maddy, cheeks pink, a calf-length black coat belted around her waist, a matching handbag over one shoulder. She had a red scarf knotted around her neck and on her head was a black knit hat.

She was dressed for Cambridge in winter. And that fact made him smile as he stepped aside to let her in. Except her glance went immediately to his desk, probably looking for the same picture he'd been staring at. Guilt gnawed at him all over again.

"I'm ready if you are," she said.

"Yes. More than ready. Just let me get my coat."

"Is Ivy okay?"

"She's fine for now. Judy has promised to look in on her in case we're late."

Something about the way the words came out made him stiffen. They weren't some normal couple going out on the town. And they never would be. But if he tried to correct himself it would only make things worse, so he let it stand and headed toward the exit.

Within minutes they were walking along the cobblestones of Cambridge's bustling shopping district, doing their best to dodge the scores of bicycles that whizzed by.

"It always seems strange that there are so few cars."

"It's a university city. Can you imagine trying to navigate through here by car with all the bikes and pedestrians?" He grabbed her hand and hauled her close to avoid another cyclist. She laughed, pulling the strap of her bag higher on her shoulder.

Tiny shops dotted either sides of the streets, which were still full of shoppers trying to get their Christmas gifts. Although the Christmas lights hadn't yet been turned on, they were everywhere, strung from one side of the street to the other, the center of each set sporting a large star. And there were Christmas trees everywhere. In the evenings, after the shops were closed, it was a beautiful sight and one that sent a reminder punch straight to his gut. Here he was out here thinking about what the town looked like at night, while Ivy was stuck in a hospital bed.

"It's gorgeous." Maddy's face was tilted up toward the peaked roofs and the varying facades along the route.

"The town? Or the decorations?" He looped her hand through the crook of his arm, the act seeming far too natural, the pressure of her fingers curling around him sending a warmth through his chest. He was just trying to keep from losing her.

He swallowed. Losing her?

She glanced at him, pushing her hat more firmly onto her head before shoving her free hand into the pocket of her coat. "Both. I can appreciate the beauty of the season, even if Christmas itself leaves me cold. Pun unintended."

"Point taken. So where to first?"

"I'm looking for a dress and probably shoes. I think my handbag will suffice. And you?"

"A tie, and since I didn't think to bring my suit to the hospital with me I probably need to buy one."

She paused and glanced down the street. "So where is the best place to find those?"

"Probably one of these shops. If you're up for walking a bit, we can just window shop until something grabs your attention. It won't take more than about half an hour to see all of it."

"Ha! I'm not the biggest shopper in the world, but I suspect it'll take me a little longer than that."

He had to smile at the way her eyes took everything in. The half-timbered buildings, their creamy white masonry filling in the areas between dark wooden beams. The durable streets that had held up for generations and which now gleamed in the sunlight. The old-world charm of life and a way of living that had been honed over the centuries.

Things that Theo took for granted but were probably new to someone used to a different way of life. Trying to see it through her eyes, a sense of pride enveloped him. He loved this city, he always had, which was why he'd chosen to stay here and build a thriving hospital. It was also a university city, teeming with young people who brought a life and intensity that wasn't found everywhere.

"Can I go in here?"

Theo glanced at the shop next to them and frowned. "I don't think you'll find a dress in there. Just some odds and ends."

"It's okay. I'll just be a minute."

She didn't wait for an answer, just disappeared inside. He wasn't sure whether he should go in after her or just wait for her to re-emerge. He had no idea what she could possibly want here. It was kind of an artsy shop with handcrafted home items. Maybe she wanted a gift for a friend. Within ten minutes she came out with a small package.

"Did you find what you wanted?"

"I did. Thanks for waiting." She didn't enlighten him as to what she'd purchased. Or for whom. She didn't have family, according to what she'd told him. But surely she had friends back in the States.

They walked a bit further and Theo spied a shop that had semi-formal wear for both men and women. "This looks like a likely place."

"Great."

They went in, shedding their winter coats and hanging them on hooks just inside the door. "It looks like dresses are down here, but I don't see any menswear."

"It's upstairs. How much time do you need?"

"Not long."

When he gave her a skeptical look, she smiled. "That looks like a challenge to me. I bet I can find something in less than a half-hour. How about if the last person back has to…?" Her lips puckered in a way that caught his attention and held it. The pucker turned into teeth catching one corner of her bottom lip and holding it for a second or two.

Hell, he could think of a great punishment for being last, but it probably wasn't one that would go over very well with her. Or with him, for that matter.

"The last person back has to…to choose the gift for the bride and groom," she finally said.

"Gift?" Something inside sagged in disappointment. Okay, had he really expected her to come up with something personal? No. But a part of him had been making up possible scenarios, as unlikely as it was that any of those would ever come to pass.

"Do you not buy wedding gifts here?" Her face tilted to look at him, and it might have been his imagination, but he thought he caught the slightest hint of laughter in her tone. Had she somehow read his thoughts and found them hilarious?

No, there was no way she could know. "Are you sure you didn't already buy a wedding gift back at that last shop?"

The laughter faded in an instant. "I'm positive."

So whatever she'd bought couldn't be mistaken for a gift for a bride and groom.

He shook off his thoughts. "Okay. Let's see who finishes first."

"You're on."

They took off in opposite directions, Theo going for the stairs. And although he didn't think they were really racing, he'd never been much of a shopper. He was pretty content with going in and finding what he needed and getting back out. But he also wasn't thrilled about having to choose a gift for Marco and Alice, since he had no idea what they might like or need. So he took his time looking through the racks of suits before finding a black one that he liked.

Then he remembered he'd said he would try to match his tie to Maddy's dress, which now sounded like an idiotic idea. It wasn't like she was his prom date or anything. But Marco had made a point of telling him what the wedding colors were, so it stood to reason that photographs would be taken. They would at least want everyone coordinated a little bit. A black suit, though, he couldn't go wrong there. He found his size and tried it on and deemed it suitable. Then he got dress shoes, a white shirt, and a few other items, paying for them and waiting while they were loaded into a shopping bag.

Then he headed downstairs where he spied Maddy, looking through the racks of dresses.

"Did you already find a suit?"

"I did. Are you having any luck?"

She looked up, brows raised as if in surprise. "I've been done for fifteen minutes."

"You're kidding."

"Nope." She reached down to lift a matching bag and laughed. Probably at the shell-shocked expression on his face. "I tend to be a bit competitive," she said.

"I guess so. I still need to get a tie. What color dress?"

"Green. If we go up and look at them, I can help pick one out."

Ten minutes later, she'd chosen a tie in a deep spruce color with a subtle patterning that only showed up when the light hit it a certain way. "Marco said she was using ivy in her bouquet, so that's what I went with."

"Christmas colors, since she's also using red roses."

"That's what I thought as well." She smiled. "So what are you going to get them as a present?"

"Cash?"

"What?" There was enough outrage in her voice that it was his turn to laugh.

"I'm kidding. But, seriously, I have no idea."

"Hmm. Marco said they're flying off to Italy right after they get married, so maybe something to do with their trip?"

"Like what?"

"I don't know. I thought maybe we could walk a little more and see if something strikes our fancy."

He glanced at Maddy. "How long do you

need to dress, so we can plan when to arrive at the hotel?"

"Judging from our shopping times, I'm going to guess not as much time as you need."

"Do you compete at everything?" An image flashed through his head, making him shift. He was not going there.

"I like to win."

"That's obvious."

They bundled back up in their coats.

"I think I have an idea about a present that might work." She ducked out onto the street and was almost lost from sight. The shoppers had increased in number and it took a little bit of maneuvering to reach her. He reached for one of her mittened hands, smiling when she curled her fingers around his. "I thought I was going to be swept downriver for a second. This is fun. You were right. I did need to get away from the hospital for a while."

"I think we both did."

Maddy stayed close to his side as they wandered down the road and turned into another alley. "I can't seem to find what I want."

When she adjusted her purchases for the third time, he took the bag from her and added it to his own. "What were you thinking of?"

"A set of bright matching luggage tags. It was something I wished I'd had when I came, since it's hard to pick out your luggage sometimes on the carousels."

"I like it."

"I hope they do too. I'm just not sure where to…"

He tugged her hand and started back the way they had come. "Actually, the shop you went in at first has all kinds of unique items. I think they carry handmade luggage as well. And it's on the way back to the hotel."

"Perfect."

Arriving back at the shop a few minutes later, they found a set of eight luggage tags in the shape of shoes. High heels. Trainers. Men's sandals. All in light tan. "The color might not stand out, but the shapes will. Silly and classy all in one package."

"I think you found a winner." And Theo thought he had too. Her no-nonsense determination and quick way of making decisions was just what they'd needed on Ivy's case. Something inside him relaxed just a bit, a feeling of hope growing instead. A hope he hadn't allowed to surface in a long time.

They had the package gift-wrapped and found a gift card that they each signed. Only afterwards did he wonder if they should have purchased separate presents, but time was growing short and he didn't want to have to explain to Maddy why it might look funny. Especially since she obviously hadn't thought so.

Taking her hand again, they headed in the direction of the hotel, a massive cream-colored building with arched entryways and a covered portico.

"Wow, this is it?"

"Yes." He had eaten here a time or two for business meetings and the inside of the hotel was just as impressive as the exterior. "They may have wanted a small wedding, but they went all out on the venue."

"I don't blame them. It's not every day you marry the love of your life." There was a wistfulness to her voice that made him pause for a second, her hand still in his.

Theo had married the love of his life once, but he wondered if that was all there was. Was one chance at love all you got? Or was there the possibility that love could reset itself with someone new?

Not something he wanted to be thinking of right now. Especially after the way he had enjoyed Maddy's company this afternoon. The way he liked the feel of her hand in his, the way her laughter trickled over him like a warm breeze sweeping through icy corridors.

They made their way up the steps with an hour to spare. They checked in at the reception desk and found a note from Marco telling them which floor they were on. Maddy was supposed to go straight to Alice's room to help her dress, while Theo was going to hole up with Marco. Knowing his friend, he would be champing at the bit to get the ceremony underway. They were a great pair, and Theo was glad they'd found happiness together. Although he'd heard rumors of the pair butting heads in the beginning, they had obviously worked out their differences.

"You go on ahead," he told Maddy, forcing himself to finally release her hand and handing her the shopping bag containing her purchases. "I want to call the hospital and check on Ivy before I go up."

"Okay, let me know if there's a problem."

He assured her he would, even though in his heart of hearts he knew there was already a problem. A big one. And it had nothing to do with Ivy and everything to do with him.

And a certain diagnostician who was rapidly capturing his daughter's heart. And, worse, she was starting to worm her way into his as well.

Oh, Lord, she wasn't sure she could do this. After helping Alice get into her dress, which was a gorgeous cream sheath dress with tiny matching flowers embroidered into the bodice and hemline, she donned her own dress, which was a lot more form-fitting than she remembered in the dressing room.

They stood there, putting the finishing touches to their make-up.

Alice put her hands on her cheeks and drew in a deep breath. "I can't believe this is happening."

Wrapping an arm around the other woman's shoulders, Madison smiled. Maybe she wasn't the only one feeling jittery, although Alice had a lot more reason than she did to be nervous. "You look gorgeous. And happy."

"I am. Marco wants to have a big ceremony with his family once we get to Italy, which is why we're opting for a small civil service here at the hotel. It doesn't matter to me where it's held, though, as long as we do it before this little one busts free." Her hand slid over her belly, which showed evidence of the life within her.

"I don't think that's going to be a problem at this point." She dropped her tube of mascara onto the countertop. "You look so beautiful, Alice."

"He makes me feel beautiful." She smoothed her dress over her hips. "I think I'm as ready as I'll ever be."

Madison scooped up the bride's bouquet and handed it to her, picking up the smaller matching one for herself. "Let's go find your groom."

"Yes, and his hunky cohort."

"Should you really be noticing the hunk factor in other men?" Madison laughed.

"Are you telling me you haven't noticed?"

"Well, I… I—"

"Joking. I'm joking, silly." Alice gave her a quick squeeze.

All of a sudden Madison was a little reluctant to see Theo. The green dress she'd bought gathered in flattering folds that fell from the waist, but it fit her upper body like a glove, thanks to the clever touch of Lycra in the fabric blend. But the saleswoman assured her it was perfect for her body type. Now she was thinking that was probably some sort of sales pitch that she would have given to anyone. Madison should have at least bought a shawl or something to wrap around herself, but as they weren't leaving the hotel—at least she didn't think they were—she'd figured she would be fine. And her dress had long sleeves, even though it was off the shoulder.

They were supposed to meet the men in the room the hotel had set up for civil ceremonies. As they entered the lobby, a couple of men turned to look as they walked by. Frowning, Madison wrapped her arms around her waist, a little irritated with herself for being as self-conscious as she was. She was normally able to block out anything and walk with her head held high, no matter how squirmy she might feel inside.

"There." Alice practically flew down the short set of stairs that led to the lower level of the lobby, forcing Madison to hurry to keep up. Too late, she spotted Marco and Theo waiting at the bottom, both in black suits. Theo's eyes were glued to her as she slowed her steps, making her even more unsure of her choice in dresses. Marco swept his soon-to-be bride up and twirled her around, while Theo kept his hands behind his back. But his face told another story, a wave of color moving up his neck, a pulse beginning to throb in his right temple.

When she reached the ground level, he moved forward, leaning over to whisper, "*That* is the dress you got?"

Oh, God, did he think it was unprofessional of her to wear something like this? They *were* off the clock, so why would he even care? "Is there something wrong?"

"Yes. But not with your dress. Or with you."

She had no idea what he meant, but he didn't sound upset. Just surprised, if she had to guess from his voice.

"Your suit looks nice."

And it did. His black jacket hugged his broad shoulders in a way that made her mouth water, and the crisp white shirt and tie looked like something he'd wear to a swanky restaurant to negotiate deals and conquer competitors. So did his proud bearing.

"Doesn't Madison look lovely?"

She blinked back to awareness, realizing that Marco and Alice had joined them, arms locked around each other's waists. Alice stared at Theo expectantly.

"Yes. She looks quite…er…nice."

Ha! He could have been speaking about his sister. Or an acquaintance, for that matter.

But wasn't that all they were? Acquaintances?

A thought that sent her stomach spinning to her feet.

"Do you have the little gift we got for them?" Madison asked to cover the awkwardness of the moment.

"Yes." Theo reached into the inner pocket of his suit jacket and produced a small gift-wrapped package, which he handed to Alice. "We hope this is something you can use."

Even though she'd used "we" a second ago, his use of it made her stomach pick itself up off the floor.

"Thank you for everything, especially coming down here on such short notice." Marco smiled. "You both clean up quite well."

Thanks to a little last-minute shopping.

The hotel lobby was just as gorgeous as the outside, boasting a huge Christmas tree that rivaled the two at Hope Hospital. Greenery wound down the staircase and dripped from every arched opening. It was a magical atmosphere, even with the tourists that were snapping pictures everywhere.

"You both look stunning as well," Madison said. "How does it feel to be getting married?"

"Like a dream come true." Alice looked up at her groom with a smile. "I am so ready to do this. But first open their present, Marco."

The groom slid the ribbon off the little box and slipped his finger beneath the paper, popping the tape with ease. Alice moved in close to watch as he removed the top. Then he grinned and held up a high-heeled luggage tag. "This is going to look great on the handle of my briefcase."

"Ha-ha." Alice grabbed it from him. "This one is mine. It looks like you have plenty of others to choose from."

She lifted another shoe, a trainer this time. "How about this one?"

"That's more my style, although I'm sure the first one would be a great ice-breaker at parties. Thank you both. They are obviously going to get a lot of use in the very near future." He put the top back on, ignoring Alice's protest to look at the rest of them.

"Getting cold feet?" Marco teased her.

"After it took this long to get you all straightened out? I don't think so."

They made their way to the room set aside

for the ceremony and, like the rest of the hotel, it was tastefully decorated with flowers and greenery, but this time there was less emphasis on Christmas, since not everyone celebrated that holiday. The official was already there behind a little desk, filling out some forms. He looked up.

"Baxter, Ricci?"

"Yes, that's us."

Standing, he said, "Are you ready to get started?"

They exchanged paperwork and the man glanced up at Theo and Madison. "You're the witnesses?" When Theo nodded, he said, "If you could sign the documents immediately after the ceremony I would appreciate it."

Surprisingly, what could have been a dry, cold reciting of vows was anything but. The official had a warm, reassuring voice and a way of moving them along from one thing to the other that was seamless. Madison stood next to Alice and took her bouquet when it was time to exchange the rings.

When she happened to glance up, Theo was watching her, a slight frown on his face that could have meant anything. She lifted her brows in question, only to have him give

her a slight smile and an almost impercep-
tible shake of his head.

She had no idea what that meant either.

And then Alice and Marco were officially
married and all the papers signed. "Time to
throw the bouquet."

Madison looked around in horror, but of
course there was no one else. "That's not necessary."

"Nope, it will be bad luck not to. And I've
had enough of that to last a lifetime. Time for
a brand-new start."

Marco kissed her cheek. "Absolutely."

"Please?" Alice asked her. "It's all in good
fun."

Good fun?

Almost before the words were out of her
mouth, something came sailing through the
air. Madison's instincts kicked in and she
grabbed at it.

Alice laughed. "See? No harm."

No harm?

Madison looked anywhere but at Theo. It
was just a game, like Alice had said. No need
to be embarrassed or act like she was taking
this thing seriously.

She pressed the bouquet back into the

bride's hands. "You'll want to have this pre-served."

They hugged. "I can't believe how happy I am. Thank you for making this day even more special."

The air around them seemed to change, negative ions transformed by the power of love. "Do you guys mind if we slide away?" Marco glanced at Alice. "Our flight leaves the day after tomorrow and we have a ton of things to do."

Sure they did. Madison couldn't hold back her smile, squeezing Alice's hand one more time. "Of course we don't. Have a wonderful trip and we'll see you when you get back."

Marco shook Theo's hand. *"Grazie."*

"You're very welcome. Enjoy married life."

There was a wistfulness behind the words that made her heart twist. Thinking about Hope and the life they'd shared?

"I intend to cherish every moment with my *tesoro*." Marco smiled, then leaned in and said something in a low voice to Theo, pressing something into his hand. Something that made Theo frown.

What was that all about?

There was no time to ask since Alice was already saying her goodbyes. A few seconds later the couple walked away, sharing a kiss or two as they went.

Madison sighed. "That was beautiful. They make a great couple."

"Yes, they do." He came to stand beside her. "Would you like to take a walk? We were in such a hurry trying to get things together for the wedding, that I don't think you really got to enjoy the city. Besides, now that it's dark, the lights will be on. Do you want to change first?"

"Oh, I forgot, my things are still up in Alice's room!" She had no idea how she was going to get them, and she didn't want to burst in on anyone.

"No, they aren't. Marco is moving them over to the room he used when we were getting dressed. He said it was ours to use."

Her eyes widened and he must have realized how that sounded because he added gruffly, "To get dressed in, of course."

Embarrassment zipped up her abdomen at having him read her so well. "Of course."

"Are you okay with walking through town a bit more?"

She hesitated, not sure at all that that was the smartest thing to do, but knowing she didn't want tonight to end. It had been the best evening she'd had in Cambridge so far. So with gratitude in her heart for the brief respite from all the crazy hours at the hospital, she said, "I'd like that very much."

# CHAPTER SEVEN

HE WASN'T SURE what had prompted him to ask Maddy to take a walk. But he wasn't sorry he had. When she'd glided down those stairs earlier, he had been floored by his reaction. It hadn't been the dress, although that was something right off the cover of some fashion magazine. With her long limbs and delicate features, she could easily be featured there as well.

Something about that simple wedding and Maddy's rapt face as she'd watched the bride make her vows had been…magical. A couple of times she'd caught him staring at her and had lifted a brow in a way that had cranked his engine and got his motor running. She knew. Or did she?

No matter how hard he'd tried to fix his attention straight ahead after that, his gaze had kept shifting back millimeter by millimeter until it had been on her again.

His motor was still running, and all he knew was that he wanted to show her off a little—a purely male reaction that was impossible to completely suppress. And right now he didn't want to even try.

He glanced at her feet. "Are you going to be okay walking in those over the uneven streets?"

"We're not going to be power walking, are we?"

"No. Strolling. And not terribly far. It just seemed like a festive night to walk under the lights. Besides, it's a shame to have spent all that time getting ready just to emerge from the hotel in our everyday clothes."

"Like Cinderella," she murmured.

"Not planning on running out on me at the stroke of midnight, are you?"

"Nope. No mad dash to a pumpkin carriage for this girl."

"You'll need a coat, though. I'll go up and get them."

By the time he got back, she was looking out of the hotel window. He dropped her black coat around her shoulders and handed her her hat and gloves.

"Thank you."

He'd discarded his suit jacket for his thicker wool coat, and couldn't resist taking her hand like he had earlier. To keep from losing her, he insisted to himself.

They walked along in silence, taking in the sights.

"I'd forgotten how chilly it was."

"Do you want to go back?"

"No. Let's walk for a few more minutes, please. It's a beautiful night."

Letting go of her hand and turning her toward him, he buttoned the top button of her coat and wrapped her scarf around her a little tighter. "Better?"

"Yes."

Something about bundling her up against the elements made a rush of warmth flow through his chest. He…cared.

About her. About whether or not she was cold.

Damn. This was getting out of hand. He needed to stop mooning over things that could never be.

That didn't stop him from sliding an arm behind her back and keeping her close by his side, though. Something any friend would do.

*Right, Theo. Keep telling yourself that.
Maddy is not your friend.*

That was the problem. He didn't know what she was. Didn't have an easy category to file her under.

She seemed to snuggle closer, the arm that had been holding the collar of her coat closed slipping around his waist. He liked the feel of her pressed tight against him. It felt…right.

And Theo had no idea how he felt about that, especially after all that had happened over the last couple of weeks.

It had to be the recent spate of romantic unions around the hospital with Ryan and Evie, Finn and Naomi and now Marco and Alice all finding someone to love.

Was he just lonely?

He hadn't felt the need to be with anyone for almost five years. Why now?

There was no answer for any of those questions.

"Are the university students all going home for the holidays? It's busier than I expected at this time of year."

"It's always busy. Most of the students have gone home, though, although some have flats and stay year-round. King's College, where the carol service will be held, isn't far from here."

Maddy hadn't mentioned the ticket since he'd given it to her. She'd acted like she wasn't interested in going because of her ambivalence over Christmas. But she seemed to be enjoying the lights in the town center. "Does it make you uncomfortable to be out looking at the lights? We can go somewhere else if you'd like."

"No, they're beautiful. I can separate the beauty from the more personal traditions. That's the part I'm not crazy about."

He walked a few more steps, wondering if it was any of his business. But he couldn't stop the question. "Because of your mum."

"Yes. It's easier now. But when I was growing up, I hated receiving Christmas presents because there was only one thing I wanted back then. To be reunited with my mom." Her shoulder moved against his side as she shrugged. "That never happened. And now as an adult I know why. She died."

"I can understand that. After Hope died, I did my best to keep things going and to make Christmas special for Ivy, but for me personally..."

The arm around him tightened. "I get it.

Really I do." She sighed as they came to the far edge of the buildings. "But look at that sky up there. Those are the best lights of all. And they're up there all year. No need to put them up or take them down."

Looking up to where a bit of sky was visible, the night was unusually clear and cloud-free, and a few stars were indeed shining, like a small collection of twinkle lights. "There's a better view from Castle Hill if you want to walk there."

"I'm fine right where I am."

Theo felt warm, and happy. And he realized he was fine right where he was too.

Maybe she wasn't the only one who'd needed to get away. Ivy's illness had taken a toll on him, with one day running into the next. Tonight would stand out in his memory as one of the few bright spots during a time of chaos and uncertainty. Could this be the turning point? They would go back to the hospital rested and refreshed and find that breakthrough in her condition they'd been looking for?

Christmas was supposed to be a time of miracles. Maybe he would even find his.

God, he hoped so.

"Are you sure you're warm enough, Maddy?"

"Yes." There was a pause. "Not many people call me Maddy anymore. Not since my mom left."

He blinked. He'd been thinking of her by the shortened version of her name for a week now. He'd never stopped to wonder if it might bother her. "I'm sorry. Would you prefer me not use it?"

"No. I actually like it." She laughed. "As long as everyone else at the hospital doesn't suddenly start calling me that."

So he was the only one allowed to call her Maddy? His stomach did a flip, and he stopped and turned her toward him, his arm still around her. He looked into her face, noting her nose was tipped with red because of the chill. And she was gorgeous. More than gorgeous, because her beauty wasn't only skin deep. "Have I told you how lovely you look tonight?"

Her head tilted back and strands of her hair brushed over the top of his hand. He couldn't resist opening his fingers to let the silky locks sift between them.

"You look pretty good yourself. And thank you for tonight. You could have just let me muddle through the shops and find the hotel by myself. But it was a lot more fun doing it with you."

"Was it?" He smiled, his fingers moved higher, closing over her hair this time and tugging slightly.

"Mmm… Yes. I feel deliciously relaxed and mellow. Even if my feet are starting to grumble a bit."

His smile grew. "I would offer to lend you mine, but I don't think they would be any more comfortable. Shall we go back?"

"Do we have to?"

She linked her hands behind his back, sending his thoughts sliding a little further down a dark road that held wonders…and dangerous curves. Much like the ones that were currently pressed against him.

"We should, yes." Something in him urged him to say what he was thinking. None of them had forever. Hope's death had shown him that. Sometimes you just had to take those bits of joy where you could find them, *while* you could find them. That didn't mean he had to demand forever, or the kind of promises that Marco and Alice had shared.

"I guess you're right." She sounded so despondent that he smiled.

"That doesn't mean tonight has to end

just yet." He leaned down and slid his cheek against hers, the chill in her skin making him yearn for warm covers and even warmer bodies.

"My apartment?"

"There's always the hotel. Marco gave us his room, remember? It's booked until morning."

She blinked, looking into his eyes. "And our things are still there, after all, so we do have to get them."

And then do what?

Go out to eat? Or stay *in* to eat.

"What are you thinking?" He needed things spelled out so he could prepare for disappointment if he'd misunderstood her intentions.

"That I don't want this night to end. Not yet." She pressed her face to his chest. "And, like you said, maybe it doesn't have to."

"Are you suggesting what I think you're suggesting?"

"That we utilize Marco's gift? Yes."

A sudden sense of rightness came over him, although he had no idea why that was. Maybe it was just relief at having the decision made. "Are you sure about this?"

"No, but in my line of work, sometimes

you just have to go with your gut. And my gut is telling me to let loose and do something dangerous tonight. I can play it safe tomorrow."

"Being with me is dangerous?" Something shimmered just below the horizon, a need that he was going to have a hard time extinguishing, if things took a wrong turn.

She leaned up and bit his chin. "You are the epitome of dangerous."

"Well, lady, so are you. I vote Marco's room." He reached into his pocket and held up an entry card. "He gave me the key."

Somehow they made it back to the hotel, via a late-night chemist to buy protection, but the memory of actually walking there was a bit foggy. It was like they'd coasted along, peppered with small touches of the hand, a palm pressed against her back, a moment spent kissing beside a brightly lit Christmas tree. The journey was winding toward its final destination. And Theo was having a hard time believing this beautiful, kind, intelligent woman actually wanted to be with him.

He knew he wasn't the same person he used to be. Cynicism had become his calling card. Oh, he hid it from patients well enough, but those who knew him well? They'd seen the changes and were warier around him than they used to be.

There. The front doors of the hotel. Finally.

As long as they didn't run into the newlyweds, they were fine, not that they would. Alice and Marco weren't likely to come out of their room, and neither were he and Maddy.

No need to let Judy or the hospital know he'd be a little bit later than he'd planned. He wouldn't be spending the night at the hotel. Just…a few hours. He hoped.

Soon they were on their way to their fourth-floor room. The elevator had several people in it, but Theo couldn't resist slinging his arm around her shoulder. He wanted—no, he *needed* to touch her.

He glanced at the electronic door key in his hand as they got off on their floor. Room 423. To the left, according to the sign on the wall and his own memory. He took her hand and headed halfway down the corridor. The key unlocked the door with a slight snick, a green light displayed on the reader. Theo pushed through the solid barrier and reentered a room that was on par with what he would expect of a hotel of this caliber.

"It's gorgeous. A little different from the one Alice was in."

Maddy's soft words were filled with wonder as she came out from behind him to survey the space. The huge bed sported a brown damask coverlet that was puffy in a way that could only mean it was filled with the finest down. The walls went along with the style of the city around them, dark bare timbers interspersed with white plaster walls, more beams crisscrossing the high ceilings.

"I know something that's even more gorgeous." He waited for her to turn and look at him. "Are you glad you came?"

Her eyes met his, shining with something he was afraid to examine. Then she came over and took his face in her hands, her thumb brushing over his lower lip in a way that made him see stars that were even brighter than those in the night sky. "So very glad."

That did it for him. He leaned down and took her mouth, one arm going behind her back and dragging her against him. Soon their surroundings were put out of mind as his hands went to her shoulders, barely able to believe she was his to explore without fear. Without worrying that someone would come upon them and see them.

Without worrying about what tomorrow was going to bring.

Live dangerously, that was what she'd said.

It had been so long since he'd lived like that, or had dwelled in the land of here and now. And he was ready to. With her.

No fears of forever. Or, worse, the lack of them.

Maddy would be going home when her time in England was over. He could kiss her, lie naked with her. Lose himself in her.

Without losing *himself.*

At least that was what he hoped. What he needed to believe.

He didn't have to ease her toward the bed, she was already moving there on her own. Slowly stepping backward and coaxing him to come with her with tiny kisses that he couldn't quite deepen without following her. Not that he minded.

She half turned him and pushed, the pressure of the bed at the backs of his knees causing them to buckle. But he sat, rather than allowing himself to fall flat on his back. And when he did so he reached and found the hem of her dress and eased it up, his palms gliding up the soft creamy skin at the back of her thighs. Leaning forward, he pressed his lips to her belly, knowing he was going to kiss her there once he'd rid her of her clothes. Then he was going to press his lips against every inch of that gorgeous body. "Come up here with me."

She blinked at him as if not sure what he was asking, so he used light pressure just beneath her bottom to tell her what he wanted.

Straddling his legs, she came onto the bed, her knees on either side of his thighs. He hugged her close, feeling the sweet pressure of her coming to rest against an area of his body that had been dying for this for what seemed like forever.

"Maddy. *Hell*." He wrapped an arm around the curve of her behind and tugged her tight against him, her slight exhalation washing over his cheek.

He wanted it like this. Just like this. With her rising and falling above him and taking him into the clouds.

As if she knew exactly what he was thinking, she slid down him, still fully clothed, but she might as well have taken him inside her. This was it. The moment they'd been heading toward for two weeks.

Her eyes shut tight, lower lip pursed as she moved against him again. Taking his hands from their perch, he trailed them up her spine until he reached the top edge of her dress, which was just off her shoulders. Tucking his fingers beneath it, he coaxed the stretchy fabric down inch by inch until it slid over her breasts. Breasts that were contained in a whisper-thin layer of lace. Peach. The color of her skin. A peekaboo effect that he couldn't resist.

Leaning her back slightly, he moved in and closed his mouth over the tight ridge visible at the center of the cup. The nipple was tight and exquisite, and he pulled on it, lapping his tongue over the fabric-covered mound.

Her hands went to his shoulders and she pushed herself closer, and a low whimper was followed by a rub of friction to the front of his trousers. He hadn't lost control while fully clothed since he was a teenager, but there was a real danger right now that he was going to fly over the edge.

He didn't want to do that without taking her with him. So he held her hips still while he continued to tug and kiss and lick, until he could stand it no longer.

"Take it off," he whispered, afraid to let go of her.

Her hands left his shoulders long enough to

reach behind her back and unhook the strapless bra, letting it fall to the side of the bed. Then she was bare to him, except when he went to take her in his mouth, she leaned away from him.

"Your turn."

Denied of his prize, he frowned. "What do you mean?"

She climbed off the bed and said. "Unzip them."

He hesitated, noting the lift of her brows.

"Unzip. Them."

Then she did the unthinkable. She reached under her dress and did something. When her hands came back up, there was a lacy strip of cloth that matched the bra.

He cursed softly.

"That makes two things I've given you in exchange for..." She leaned forward, her palms gliding along his shoulders, breasts tantalizingly close to his mouth. "Unzip your trousers."

One nipple trailed across the seam of his lips and he immediately closed over it, giving a long hard pull that he thought would alleviate some of the growing pressure from behind that zipper. It didn't. It just ratcheted things up until they were at boiling point. He was going to lose it, and it was either with her or without her.

He reached down and grabbed the tab on the fastener and slid it down, undoing the button afterwards. Then he reached in and freed his aching flesh. But not without biting down on her nipple.

She moaned and arched in, before climbing back on the bed, her dress tugged up.

Then they were flesh to flesh, and he was pretty sure this was where it would end. But it didn't. He cupped her face, moving her within kissing distance. And kiss her he did. The way he'd wanted to that first time. Tongue and teeth and snatched breaths, the building of an empire that was going to explode long before he was ready.

Expertly whipping a condom on, Theo lifted her slightly, but she was already anticipating, reaching for him and positioning herself. Then she engulfed him in heat. In sweet, sweet heaven. Taking him to a world where everything was tight and wet and filled with a pleasure beyond anything he could imagine.

It had never been like this before.

Not even with Hope.

A bright flash of guilt stabbed through him. He gripped her hips and urged her to move, needing to squeeze out everything that didn't involve Maddy. And what she was doing to him.

God. She did it for him.

Her fingers pushed into his hair and gripped the strands as she continued to ride him, holding his face against her shoulder as her breathing roughened.

He wasn't going to last. And he didn't want to. But he also didn't want to go without her. Holding tight to her hips, he lay back until his shoulders touched the mattress, and then he watched. Watched her rise and fall. Watched his erection disappear inside her.

So close.

Pressing a palm against her lower belly, he followed her rhythm, his thumb dipping in and discovering the tiny bud he was searching for. He circled it, touching and not quite touching in at random intervals.

She moaned, a long low sound that was half need and half frustration. But he wasn't quite ready to finish her yet. He wanted to wait. Wanted her to wait. Until they were both ready—until they were wound so tight they were ready to snap—to break into a million pieces.

"Theo," she panted. "Please."

The plea didn't fall on deaf ears. He touched her, applying steady pressure that increased every time she reached the bottom of a stroke. He hoped the little jolt of pleasure would match his own each time her body took him all the way in.

It evidently did, because her eyes slammed shut and she increased the speed and the force of her thrusts as he struggled to hold on.

Just a little. Hell, just give me a little more...

Maddy's body slammed all the way down, and her breath whooshed from her as a strong series of contractions hit him and blew him away.

That was it. Her eruption became his, and he came harder than he'd ever come in his life, the squeeze of her body forcing his to give everything it had.

Until it was done.

Over.

Tiny ripples still quaking his center, he wrapped his arms around her and pulled her down against him, careful to remain connected. He just needed a few more seconds. A few more whispers of sensation.

Her head nestled in the crook of his neck as he waited for the waves to carry him back to the shore. It wasn't all at once. They pushed him forward and then dragged him back for what seemed like forever, their breath mingling, her hair tickling his chest.

He kissed her cheek.

Tonight was something he would never forget. Would never forget her.

Ever.

There was something final about that word. Something that tugged at a place inside him that was long forgotten. Or was it just buried too deep to be found?

Whatever it was, he was changed.

Marked.

With that realization came a niggle of fear. They were in a hotel room that didn't belong to them, doing something they—

What was he doing here?

He firmed his jaw. Nothing they both hadn't wanted.

She hadn't asked for forever. Hadn't even hinted at it. Which was good.

Wasn't it?

He had no idea.

Maddy shifted for a second, and he thought she was going to pull away and get dressed. He wasn't quite ready for that yet. Wanted a few more seconds to figure this out.

"Don't leave."

She sat up to look at him. "I wasn't going to. My legs are just going to sleep."

He smiled. "We can't have that, can we?"

Moving to the center of the bed, he pulled down the covers and motioned for her. "Lie with me. Just for a few minutes."

A few minutes turned into a few hours of watching her sleep. For real this time. Without fighting it. And then unable to do anything else, he blanked everything out except for the feel of her warmth against him, the soft steady sound of her breathing.

*Almost* paradise?

The song had it so very wrong.

She *was* paradise. And now that he'd had a taste of it, he wasn't sure he could let it go. No one else would ever come close to where this woman had taken him tonight.

And he didn't want them to.

All he wanted was her.

It scared the hell out of him, but there was absolutely nothing he could do to change it. And he wasn't sure he would, even if he could.

He could worry about that tomorrow. But for the next couple of hours he was going to enjoy having her close, because who knew better than he did that tomorrow wasn't promised? Not to him. Not to Maddy.

Not to anyone.

Maddy opened her eyes and found darkness. But there was sound.

Something.

A ringtone. But it wasn't hers. It was unfamiliar.

A spot of light appeared, and then a low masculine voice abruptly cut the sound off, speaking into the phone.

Then another one went off, one she recognized this time, and a frisson of fear woke her up the rest of the way. She remembered exactly where she was. Who she was with. And what that call might be about. There was no way both of their phones could go off at once, unless...

*Ivy!*

Stumbling through the darkness, she searched for her phone just as Theo belted out, "When?"

She found hers. "Hello?"

"Madison, this is Naomi. Ivy has taken a turn. We're trying to locate Theo, but so far no luck. You wouldn't happen to know where..." A pause was followed by "What?"

to someone nearby. Then her friend came back on the line. "Okay, Dr. Sumner has found him. Sorry to bother you. But do you think you could come in? I know it's late." Out of the corner of her eye she saw Theo grabbing for his clothes, his muscles flashing in the low light of her phone.

"Of course. What's going on?"

"Ivy woke up crying." Naomi's swift indrawn breath told her this was about something far worse than a simple nightmare or bellyache. She waited for her friend to continue.

"Madison. She can't feel her legs. At all."

"I'm on my way."

Ending the call, she tossed her phone on the bed and looked for her own clothes. Not the ones from the wedding but her normal street clothes.

They were still in the bags on the floor. She hurried over and dragged them out, then realized she still needed to locate her panties, which were somewhere in that huge bed. She scrambled onto it, tossing aside bedclothes and sheets, until she found them buried beneath the rubble.

Rubble. That was a very good word to describe the aftermath of last night. Guilt snaked up her spine, lodging at the base of her skull.

Theo still hadn't said a word as he sat on the edge of the bed and pulled on his socks and shoes. She dragged on bra and panties, unable to face him naked, then she turned on the light, blinking until her eyes adjusted. "Was that Dr. Sumner?"

"Yes." The one-word answer was curt with pain and accusation. Probably not at her but at himself.

She went to stand over by him. "This isn't your fault."

"Hell if it's not. I never should have been in this room." He glanced up at her, angry eyes skating down her body and then away. The inference was obvious.

It was like a slap to the face.

*He's hurting. This is not about you.*

She could tell herself that for as long as she wanted, but it didn't change the fact that he regretted being here with her. Making love to her.

If it could even be called that. Right now he'd looked at her as if he loathed her.

Maybe he did. But probably not more than he loathed himself.

She gathered the rest of her clothes and pulled them on, not bothering with her coat.

When he spoke again, his voice was devoid of emotion. "I'll have the concierge send the rest of our things to my flat if that's okay. I'd rather not arrive with them at the hospital. In fact, I'd rather we didn't arrive together."

Her head could understand all of that. It was quite logical. But her heart cried out as yet another dart pierced her skin. He didn't want to be seen with her.

"It's fine."

It wasn't. But this wasn't about her precious ego, it was about a little girl's life.

*She can't feel her legs.*

Something about that niggled at the back of her head. Something important. But right now she couldn't separate what was what, or trust her judgement. Not until she was able to get out of this room and forget about what had happened here.

Was that even possible? Madison had no idea, but she needed to at least try.

Within fifteen minutes they had everything bagged back up and were down at the concierge's desk, where someone was ahead of them. She glanced down at her watch. Four o'clock in the morning, and there was someone else checking out? Theo looked at her. "You go on. I'll take care of this."

"No. She's your daughter. You go."

"Are you sure?"

"Yes. Just give me the address to your apartment."

Scribbling something on a piece of paper, and then handing it to her, he nodded at her. "Please don't tell—"

"I won't. Just go."

He nodded, and with a heavy sense of doom and an even heavier heart Madison watched him leave, until he was through the doors and out of sight.

Then it was just her. Alone. An all-too-familiar song in a very familiar life.

He didn't want her to tell anyone about tonight. It was obvious he had no intention of repeating what had gone on here. Even if it had rocked her world and made her realize that maybe even a lone wolf was capable of falling in—

*Stop it! This is about Ivy and not your feelings.*

The concierge could have asked any of a million questions about why the person checking out of the room was different from the person who'd checked in. But he did neither, just took down the address Theo had given her. He was polite and discreet. And for that tiny gift she was grateful.

She dragged her mind back to Ivy as she left the hotel with only her purse and the memory of all the magic she'd experienced last evening.

She couldn't feel her legs.

What did that mean?

The growing weakness had been the main symptom up until now. She assumed that if Ivy couldn't feel them, she also couldn't move them. Which meant she was now paralyzed from the waist down.

How long before that paralysis began to creep up to other affected areas.

Madison couldn't let that happen, even if she had to spend her days and nights studying every case file from here to Timbuktu.

Until she finally found one that fit Ivy's symptoms. And could put an end to her— and Theo's—agony once and for all. Then maybe, just maybe, Ivy's biggest Christmas wish might come true after all.

# CHAPTER EIGHT

"GOD, WHY DIDN'T I see it? My legs fell asleep and I didn't see the connection. Until now." She didn't care that Theo might be cringing over that particular memory. None of that mattered.

Madison bent over Ivy, retesting the sensation in her legs, and got the same result Dr. Sumner had. Nothing. Not a flinch, not a contraction of the muscle, not one hint that the nerves in her legs were transmitting signals of any type up the neural pathway. And she bet she knew why. It was the same reason she hadn't been able to feel her own legs after she and Theo had had sex. "I need an MRI. Right now."

"But you already said there were no lesions." Theo's voice was calm. Too calm as he sat by his daughter's bed.

Judy and Naomi had left the room a few

moments ago so that Madison could examine
Ivy without any distractions. Theo's housekeeper had been distraught, apologizing over
and over for falling asleep in the chair next
to the bed. It had edged Madison's guilt even
higher for keeping the child's father away
from his daughter. But if she felt guilty, then
Theo felt it a thousand times more deeply,
judging from his haggard appearance.

She remembered her earlier words to him.
*Don't you give up on me.*

It was as if he already had. As if their night
together had sounded a death knell for his
daughter.

But he was wrong. So very wrong.

Destiny was not going to punish him for
wanting—no, *needing*—a little human com-
panionship.

She felt as guilty as hell for not being here
when Ivy's symptoms had progressed. But
she wasn't going to allow her feelings to par-
alyze her—to keep from doing what needed
to be done. Unlike the times when she'd been
a kid and had sabotaged her chances in one
foster home after another, so sure her mom
was going to come back for her someday.
She'd let her emotions rule her, and they had
almost destroyed her.

Not anymore. And certainly not this time. Not when Ivy needed her. Not when Theo needed a miracle.

"I don't want another scan of her head. I want one of her back."

"Her back? I don't understand."

Ivy's voice came up to her. "What's wrong with my legs? Why can't I feel them?"

That tearful voice had asked the same question time after time ever since Madison had arrived at the hospital a half-hour earlier.

The cause had come to her in a flash. She just needed confirmation. And she prayed desperately that she was right.

She leaned in close to the child. "We're working to find out, sweetheart. Do you think you can handle being in that white tube again?"

"Y-yes. If I have to."

"It will help me find out what's going on with your legs. And hopefully make you better."

Theo's grim voice interrupted her. "Madison…"

He didn't want her to make empty promises. But she wasn't. Not this time. And if she was right…

They might be able to reverse the course

of Ivy's condition. She'd have to strengthen her muscles to be able to walk, but at least she'd have the chance to be completely mobile again.

She firmed her jaw and faced him. "I know what I'm doing. You need to trust me. In this, anyway."

He might not have trusted their decision about last night, and he'd be right. Everything about what had happened between them had been about a lack of impulse control. But here in this room she was not driven by a decision made in the heat of the moment. Or some kind of crazy attraction that had no logical basis and no possible future.

He'd as much as said it.

They hadn't checked in with the rest of the treatment team as most of them were still at home in their beds, so this was ultimately Theo's call as to whether he let her run with her hunch.

She waited with bated breath as a flurry of emotions crossed his face, and her mind wept as she read each one of them—fear, dread, guilt...pain. And finally resignation.

"Let's do it. We can talk on the way down."

Talk? Oh, God. She hoped it was about Ivy and not about last night. She didn't need anything else clogging up her thoughts. She was having enough trouble filtering pertinent information as it was.

And if he was going to try to let her down easy…

Well, it was too late. Her heart was about to crash to the earth and tear open a crater so deep that no one would ever be able to find it again. Worst of all, it was for the best.

Madison made the call to the imaging department, who said they'd send someone right up for Ivy.

She sat on the bed beside her and held her hand for a long minute, while the child looked up at her with moist blue eyes that brimmed with some of the same emotions visible on Theo's face.

"It's going to be all right. We'll be down there with you in a very few minutes, okay?"

Ivy nodded, glancing toward her father as if for reassurance.

Theo came over and kissed her on the head. "I won't leave you, sweetness. Not even for a second."

He would have to, of course. He couldn't stay in the scanning area with her, but Ivy would already know that. He could wait in the control room and talk to her, though.

Minutes later, Ivy had been whisked away, leaving Theo to explain to Judy what was going on and to ask her to wait here in the room. The housekeeper, her white hair pulled into a bun, nodded. "You'll let me know as soon as you hear anything?"

"I will."

"I'm so sorry for spoiling your evening. You made it to the wedding?"

"You didn't spoil it. And, yes, we... *I* went to the wedding. I'll call you as soon as I know something."

If Judy caught his little slip of the tongue, she said nothing, didn't even glance in Madison's direction. More hurt balled into a lump in her throat. A lump so big it was impossible to dislodge, no matter how many times she swallowed.

Madison and Theo exited the room, heading down the hallway to the elevators. "Theo, I am so sorry."

"Don't." He cut her off. "The blame lays entirely with me. If anything happens to her..."

She caught his hand, forcing him to stop. "If this is what I think it is, there's a good chance we can reverse the paralysis."

His hand tightened on hers. "What do you think it is?"

"Let's see the scans first. I don't want to jump to conclusions without seeing definitive proof. Can you wait just a little while longer?"

"I've been waiting for months, it seems. And…" a muscle in his cheek worked "…it just feels like the clock is running out."

She forced a smile. "I told you I'd tell you when to worry." She shifted her hand and linked her fingers through his, knowing she was letting her impulses reign again. But she was desperate to set his mind at ease, even though she knew it wasn't the time for that yet. "This is not it. But it is the time to hope."

He raised her hand to his lips and kissed it, sending a stream of conflicting emotions streaming through her. "I want you to be right. Heaven help me, Maddy, I pray you're right."

They sat in the room overlooking the MRI room as the machine took detailed pictures of his daughter's body section by section. She'd been given a light anesthetic to help her hold perfectly still during the process, so he was grateful that she wasn't afraid or confused.

Unlike Theo, whose heart pounded in his chest, sending his blood pressure through the roof. It wasn't all due to Ivy either, although right now she was all that mattered.

Maddy had made Theo do something he hadn't done in a very long time. Forget about Hope.

And he damned himself for that. Damned himself that he'd been with her while his daughter had been lying in a hospital bed unable to feel her legs.

He swallowed back a sea of emotions. Even in the hallway a few moments ago, he'd been unable to resist kissing her hand.

As a result of her words, his conscience argued.

No. As a result of last night. And it had to stop. Right here. Right now. Nothing else was going to divert his energy from finding out what was wrong with Ivy. Not even Maddy.

Especially not Maddy.

He'd had no trouble brushing off a woman's interest. Up until now. And the worst part of it was the interest hadn't started with her. It had started with him. He'd been the one who'd felt an immediate attraction to her. And he still had no idea why.

Yes, she was funny and sweet and tenacious as hell when it came to her patients. And she was beautiful beyond belief. But for him to have let down his guard at a time when it should have been at its highest was unforgivable. If Hope knew he'd jeopardized their daughter's health on a night of meaningless sex, she'd be horrified.

Only he wasn't so sure it had been meaningless. And that horrified *him*. He'd been so sure that no one would ever be able to take his late wife's place. And here he was pining over a flesh-and-blood woman who was here, whereas Hope wasn't.

"Okay. That should do it." The tech's voice interrupted his thoughts. "Do you want to sit with her while we read the scans?"

He was looking at Theo.

He was torn. He wanted to be with Ivy, but he also wanted to be there when the tech and Maddy scrolled through those images. He wanted to read the results on her face the moment she realized whether her hypothesis was right...or wrong.

"Can I do both? Can we go through them in the room with her?"

Maddy shook her head, her hand inching toward his before thinking better of it. "I don't think that's a good idea. I don't want her frightened if she hears us discussing the findings. I'll tell you what. Why don't you go down with her to Recovery while we look over the scans? I'll call you as soon I know something."

He had never been on this side of the equation before. He now knew how parents felt as they were forced to wait in a room while people decided what would and wouldn't happen to their child. Or debated treatment protocols and diagnoses. But he couldn't straddle the fence. Not this time. His place was with his daughter.

"Okay. But I want to know the second you have an answer."

"I'll call. I promise."

Theo left without saying another word, meeting the nurse as she wheeled the bed into one of the recovery rooms. Ivy was still sound asleep, her sweet angelic face wiped clean of any traces of worry. Or pain.

And that sent a landslide of fear through him. It was too close to how he pictured Hope's face.

He could not lose her. Surely whatever deity was up there wouldn't take her from him as well.

Hope and Ivy were the only two people he had ever really loved other than his parents.

*Really? Was that the absolute truth? Wasn't there...?*

He swallowed hard as a horrible, gut-wrenching possibility stole over him. One he shoved aside. This was not the time or the place.

And if he had his way, it would never be.

A minute later, Ivy's voice broke through. "Daddy?"

Relief swamped over him. "I'm right here, baby."

The nurse smiled at him. "She's going to be just fine. And so are you, Dad."

Ha! That was the funniest thing he'd heard all day. Only it wasn't funny. At all.

His phone chirped. He snatched it up and jabbed the talk button. "Hawkwood here."

He had no idea why he did that. He already knew from his screen that it was Maddy. Maybe the desperate need to salvage this situation and put their feet back on professional ground had forced the move.

"Um... Theo?" The confusion in her voice was plain and his gut tightened. He was a bastard. No doubt about it.

"Yes, sorry. Ivy's awake and talking."

"How are her legs?"

"I haven't asked." And he didn't want to ask. Not right now.

"Well, can you get Judy to come up and sit with her? I have something I think you'll want to see."

He gulped down a quick wash of bile. He wanted to ask her if it was a tumor or any number of catastrophic diagnoses that came to mind. But to do that would just frighten Ivy.

"Yes. Give me a minute to get her up here."

That minute seemed like hours, when in fact it didn't take long at all for Judy to speed up in the elevator and swing open that door. "How is she?"

"She's awake." He brushed Ivy's dark hair back from her face. "Judy is going to sit with you for a moment while I go and talk to Dr. Archer, okay?"

"Why are you calling her Dr. Archer, Daddy?" Ivy's tiny brows scrunched together before she gave a huge yawn. "She wants us…to call…her Madison."

She wanted him to call her Maddy. But he couldn't do that anymore. Not if he had any hope of coming out of this in one piece.

"I know she does, pumpkin. Go to sleep. I'll be back in just a little while."

He needn't have said anything. Ivy's eyelids were already heavy and sinking lower by the second. It had been a long night that had taken a lot out of them all. And dawn was beginning to relentlessly creep up over the horizon.

Judy took the seat next to the bed. "I'll be right here if she wakes."

His housekeeper had been up as long as he had, probably even longer, since he'd been busy having a good old time with Ivy's best hope for a cure.

"I'll be back as soon as I can. Thank you for everything."

"You don't need to thank me, Theo. I love this girl as if she were my own."

And since Judy had never married or had children of her own, in a very real way Ivy was like a granddaughter to her. That bond had just grown closer over the last four and a half years.

He slid from the room, closing the door with care so as not to wake Ivy. His legs carried him along, going too fast and yet feeling like he was in one of those nightmares where every step was dragged backward by some unseen force. Still he put one foot in front of the other, wanting to get there and yet not wanting to. What if there was no hope for Ivy? What if it was some incurable disease that would silently steal her away from him?

He gritted his teeth and forced himself to think of something else. She'd told him this was the time for hope, so he needed to hold onto that with all his might.

He found the tech in the scanning booth, but there was no sign of Maddy. "I have another patient coming in, sorry. Car accident victim. Dr. Archer is waiting for you in exam room one, just down the corridor and to the right."

He knew where the room was, but forced himself to thank the guy and head back out again. This time the trip was faster since the room was just around the corner.

The door was open, and Maddy was sitting inside with her back to him, her entire attention focused on the computer screen in front of her. And there it was again. That tug to his gut that appeared every time he was within ten feet of her. He'd thought spending a night with her might erase it, although it had been pure attraction that had brought them together, not a need to banish her from his system. He hadn't thought there'd been a need to do that.

Until today.

The overhead light caught the highlights in her hair, giving them a warm glow that was normally impossible with a harsh florescent tube.

His brain told him to call her by her title. His heart would not let him. Whatever else he did, he didn't want to hurt her or try to deny what had happened in that hotel room. She deserved more than that.

"Maddy?"

She whirled around on the swivel stool. When she went to push a few locks of hair behind her ears, he noticed her hand was trembling.

A cold wind blew across his soul. "What is it?"

"I can't believe I didn't see this before now. Grab that stool and sit down."

Her hand wasn't the only thing that was shaking. Her voice had a quaver to it as well. Only it didn't sound like fear. She sounded almost excited.

Was that a good thing?

He pulled the stool over from beside the

exam table and set it beside hers. "Okay. Tell me."

"I'll do better than that. I'll show you. Remember when my legs fell asleep?"

Without waiting for an answer, she began rolling her finger across the laptop's mouse pad and the images changed as quick as lightning.

"Slow down. I can't see what I'm looking at."

"Sorry. Not quite there yet." But she did as he asked and slowed the pace of the changing images as they showed the detailed snapshots of his daughter's spine, vertebrae and blood vessels.

Maddy scrolled back and forth between a couple of images before stopping abruptly. "There. What do you see?"

There was still that odd intonation to her voice that signaled urgency.

Theo peered at the images, his chaotic brain struggling to make sense of anything he was seeing. "Where am I—?"

"Here." She took her pen and pointed to an area on the screen and his world suddenly went silent.

This section of her spinal cord flowed in a smooth even line until it reached one area where it bulged out a bit. Right next to it was a tangle of blood vessels that looked… enlarged.

When he turned to glance her way, he found her staring at him. She already knew what it was. He was certain.

"Why do people's legs fall asleep?"

He swallowed, realizing now why she'd gone back to that. "Because something presses on the nerve."

"Exactly. And here it is." She circled the area. "This is what's pressing on the nerves that control her legs."

"Her veins have been causing this? The whole time?"

"Yes." She turned to look at the image again. "We'll need an angiogram to be sure, Theo, but I would bet it's an arteriovenous fistula."

"Dural?"

When she nodded, he said, "My God. It's been sitting there in plain sight all along."

Color leached from her face. "I know. I am so sorry I haven't seen it before now."

"How could you have? I would have gone months before thinking to look at the vessels near her spine, and even then it's doubtful I would have found it. Or if I had, it might have been too late to restore function. If it's not already."

"I don't think it is. A lot of these cases take a year or longer to be diagnosed. It's only been a couple of months."

"But it's progressed so fast."

Spinal dural arteriovenous fistula. He searched his memory for the condition and came up with just snatches of information. The fistula part was easy—it was an abnormal connection between two differing things. In SDAVF, the capillaries that joined arteries to veins were missing. Instead, arteries were connected directly to veins, putting a strain on them until they bulged under the increased load. Those bulges—which were slowly growing in size—put pressure on her spinal cord, resulting in damage that was hopefully reversible.

She'd said they needed an angiogram, but Theo knew she was right. The angiogram would just confirm the diagnosis and give them a definitive location, something not always visible in an MRI.

"What do we do now?"

"We get one of Hope Hospital's excellent neurosurgeons to zap those suckers and shut them down."

The way she said it, in her typical American fashion, made him laugh, although he knew part of that was the sheer force of the relief that was sweeping over him. "You did it. You told me it was a time for hope and you were right."

Before he could stop himself, he took her face in his hands and stared deep into her eyes before his gaze dropped to her lips. "I don't know how to thank you."

"Y-you don't need to thank me."

He leaned closer.

"Dr. Archer?" The sudden sound had him jerking back, sending his stool rolling several inches.

They both looked toward the door where the MRI tech was shifting from foot to foot. "I'm sorry for interrupting."

"You're not." The growled words didn't help. If anything, the young man's face turned ten shades of red before he addressed Maddy.

"Do you still want me to schedule that emergency angiogram for the patient?"

"Yes, please. And have a neurosurgeon standing by." Maddy didn't belt out the words or show emotion of any kind. She stood, smiling at the tech. "I appreciate you getting back to me so quickly."

There was something about the way she said those words that made him think she was glad the man had come in when he had.

Maybe he wasn't the only one who was having regrets over what had happened between them last night. Hell, that hadn't stopped him from swooping in on her the second they found themselves alone in a room again.

Relief. Pure and simple. He would have planted a kiss right on Judy's lips if she'd been the one to come up with the solution.

*It would have been a completely different kind of kiss, though, wouldn't it?*

Yes, it would have been.

And that's what made this situation so hard to face. He would have to get over it, though. For Ivy's sake. Once all of this was done, he could come back and dissect his feelings all he wanted but right now the only thing that was on the table was his daughter's health.

By eight in the morning the exams were all done and, as Theo knew it was going to be, Maddy's hunch was confirmed. The location of the fistula fit the area of weakness, which was mostly in her legs and creeping upward as the veins continued to swell. It was also why she suddenly had no sensation in her legs. There had probably been a rapid change in the vessels over the last couple of days. Those kinds of things could progress quickly or move forward and then plateau for a while.

Her arm weakness was probably caused by her upper body trying to compensate for her inability to use her legs to do common tasks—such as using them to shift herself or helping to move from a chair back to her bed. But that had just confused the issue, since everyone had thought it was generalized weakness over her whole body rather than it being confined to her legs.

But Maddy had found the answer. In the end, the sudden paralysis had been the key they'd needed to solve the mystery.

He was grateful. Overwhelmingly grateful. And he had no idea how to express that to her in a way that was appropriate. And the inappropriate ways were out of the question.

That was another thing he wasn't used to. He was used to being on the receiving end of his patients' gratitude. Here he was trying to sort through how to say thanks without it being just words and nothing else.

All of that could wait until Ivy's surgery

was over and she was on the mend, though. Then he would work it all out.

And decide once and for all what to do.

## CHAPTER NINE

THE SURGERY WAS a success. The neurosurgeon had performed an endovascular embolization, going in through a catheter and injecting a tiny bit of glue into the offending vessels. Like the lights on a runway going out one by one, Maddy had gotten to see the affected veins disappear off the screen as their blood flow was cut off. The body would use other—normal—veins and capillaries in the area to take over for the ones they'd just obliterated.

And hopefully as the swelling in her spinal cord subsided, Ivy would slowly regain sensation in her legs, and with hope and a lot of prayers her atrophied muscles would regain their strength. She was slated to start physical therapy in two days as soon as things started quietening down in her back.

Madison had only seen Theo for a few

minutes after the surgery. He'd seemed to be acting strangely, barely making eye contact with her before muttering a quick thank you and taking off to see his daughter.

That was understandable, though. Of course he wanted to spend every second he could with her. It was like he'd been given a new lease of life. One that matched the one Ivy had been given.

She wandered down the corridor of the surgical suite. It was midday and medical staff were flowing in and out of the rooms at a constant rate. Everything had happened so fast. She'd been up for twelve hours already.

Only twelve hours since she'd woken up in that hotel room to the sound of her cellphone ringing. It seemed like a lifetime ago. Theo had seemed to age before her eyes over the day, his sentences getting shorter and shorter. The only time she'd seen a true spark of emotion in him had been when she'd shown him the spinal dural arteriovenous fistula on the MRI scans. She could still feel his palms cupping her face as he'd leaned in to kiss her.

And he had been going to kiss her. Oh, she'd almost talked herself out of believing that, but after reliving the moment a thousand times in her head, she knew if that tech hadn't shown up when he had, Theo's mouth would have been on hers. If that had happened she'd have been just as powerless to stop her reaction to it as she'd been last night. Theo was like a tsunami. One that crashed over the walls that surrounded her heart and knocked down every defense. She'd been a willing participant.

If he asked her up to his office today or a week from today, she'd go and to hell with the consequences.

Except ever since that moment in the exam room, Theo had been the consummate professional, barely speaking to her. During surgery she'd sat in the observation area to watch. Theo had come in and had chosen a chair on the other side of the room. Her insides had squelched in embarrassment.

How could things have changed so drastically?

*You came up with the answer, that's why. He no longer needs to coddle you.*

No, Madison refused to believe that. That he'd simply been humoring her, hoping that by showing preferential treatment—hadn't he even used that expression one time?—she would work even harder on his daughter's case.

By having sex with her?

Surely not. Unless that's what he'd thought she'd wanted.

And, oh, God, she had wanted it. Had he somehow read her mind and obliged?

She swallowed. She'd gotten it in her head that in the same way Ivy was special to her, Theo was beginning to think she was special too.

But why would that even be true?

She was just a colleague. One that he'd made the mistake of sleeping with.

She had repeatedly told herself that she was not picturing Theo as anything more than a work partner. Until they'd slept together and she'd wondered if they might somehow become more than that.

A family?

Ha! Not very likely. He loved his wife. Didn't the picture that was still sitting on his desk tell her that, along with his late wife's medical degree hanging on his wall?

Maddy was a fool.

A fool who had stupidly fallen in love with a man who was unreachable.

Yes, she could finally admit it. She loved him. And it was impossible. For both of them.

She made her way to the elevator and then

to her office, wondering how she was going to finish out the last five months of her stay in England. The last thing she wanted was to run into Theo day in and day out. Unless she could somehow convince herself she didn't really love him. That working so closely together was what had done a number on her—dredging up emotions that were temporary and would fade as Ivy returned to health. As the reasons for she and Theo working so closely together came to a halt.

He was already putting the incident behind him. She could do the same.

At least she hoped she could.

And if she couldn't?

Okay, if she didn't feel more like her old self in a few weeks, she could always resign and go back to the States. It wouldn't look good on her résumé but, then again, she had never really had a stellar reputation in the human relations department. Her hospital would just think that her inability to be a team player had raised its ugly head again and gotten her thrown out.

They'd take her back. Of that she had no doubt. She may have upset some of the staff at her old hospital, but they had kept her on despite it all. And that was obviously not the result of her sparkling personality.

She smiled, feeling a little less wobbly inside. She would give it a couple of weeks and see where things stood. Then she would make her decision. This wasn't a forever job.

And it never would be.

She'd known that from the beginning. Neither would Theo swoop in and declare his undying love for her. He was in love with Hope. And that would never change.

The sooner she realized that, the better off she would be.

Madison poked her head into Ivy's room. The girl was fast asleep. Two days after surgery and all was well. For Ivy and for her.

Sensation in her legs was already returning, along with some tiny movements of her toes. All very promising signs.

Her heart contracted at who else was in Ivy's bed. Theo. Who'd spent every waking moment with his daughter, going with her to her first day of therapy this morning. She'd tried to give them as wide a berth as possible.

Until she could no longer stand it and had to see them…no, not them. Ivy. She'd tried to find a time when Theo wasn't with her, but that seemed to be never.

So she crept over to the bed to check her vitals, hoping beyond hope that she didn't wake Theo in the process. Well, if she did, she could just pretend it was a professional visit.

It was. She would make it one, even if she knew in her heart of hearts that her reasons for being here were far from professional.

Theo was on his back beside Ivy, one arm behind his head, his hand stretching to the opposite side of the bed as if keeping his daughter safe while she slept. His eyes were closed—ha! If they weren't there was no way she would be standing here right now with a lump in her throat the size of Montana.

She missed him. Missed sparring with him verbally. Missed their arguments.

Missed strolling downtown under the Christmas lights.

Most of all, she missed him holding her far into the night. Her eyes welled with tears, making it hard to see, but somehow she made her way over to Ivy's side of the bed, smiling at how small she looked in that long bed, especially next to her daddy.

She missed the little girl almost as much as she missed Ivy's father.

Firming her resolve, she slid closer so she could check her pulse and breathing.

Suddenly Ivy's eyelids flickered open, coming to focus on her.

There was no time to hide or escape to the safety of the hallway. She'd been caught creeping around like a peeping Tom.

"Mummy?"

She was evidently still half-asleep, her small hand scrubbing over her eyes in a way that made her heart break. Soon Madison would fly away and never see Ivy or her father again. There was nothing she could do about that. But she could at least make sure the parting had some closure for the little girl.

Unlike her own life, when her mother had been there one day and gone the next?

Hadn't that happened with Ivy's mom, too?

It was up to her to not add another trauma to the little girl's life. Not that she'd made that big an impact on it.

Ivy was still looking at her, and she realized she was waiting for an answer.

She forced a smile, brushing a strand of dark hair from the girl's cheek. "No. It's just me, Madison. I've come to check on you."

"I wish you were."

"You wish I was what?"

"I wish you were my mummy."

Madison's breath stalled in her lungs, her hand going to her mouth in an effort to stop the words that were clamoring to get out.

*I wish I were, too.*

The pain was almost unbearable, slashing through her again and again until she was sure there was nothing left of her heart. Her lungs. Her vital organs.

She would never get over this little girl. Or her father.

Against her will, her gaze stole over to Theo.

*Open. Open! His eyes were open!*

And he'd heard every word they'd said, his brows forming an ominous frown that chilled her to the bone. Here was one person who didn't wish she was Ivy's mother.

She had to get out of there. Now. Before he said something that brought her to her knees.

"I—I... Sorry, I was just here to make sure she was okay." She quickly said goodbye to Ivy and left the room. A second later, her back was against the wall and hot tears were splashing onto her cheeks.

Who was she kidding? She thought she

could see Theo for the next five months and act like nothing had ever happened? Act like she didn't love the man or crave him with every fiber of her being?

There was no way. And judging from the pain that still gashed and tore at her, those crazy emotions were not going away. They were only going to get worse.

"Madison? Are you okay?"

At first she thought Theo had followed her out, but it was a woman's voice. She opened her eyes to find Naomi looking at her with concern.

She reached up and scrubbed at the tears and pushed away from the wall. "I'm fine. Have you ever had one of those days where you're so exhausted you could cry? Literally?"

When Naomi gave a wary-looking nod, Madison chuckled, although it sounded more like the squawk of a pained seagull.

"Well, that's where I'm at. I was just getting ready to head home and sleep for at least eleven hours."

"Are you sure? I could drive you if you wanted."

Her friend's kind words threatened to turn the waterworks back on, so she simply shook her head. "I'm good. I'd rather walk and get some fresh air. I'll see you tomorrow."

Out of the corner of her eye, she saw the door to Ivy's room begin to open.

That was her cue to scram.

Throwing an apologetic smile to Naomi, she hurried down the corridor and didn't stop until she was in the safety of the elevator.

It was then that she knew she wasn't going back to her apartment. She was going to spend a couple of days in a hotel, during which time she was going to type up her resignation—effective immediately—and have it delivered to the hospital. Then she was going to pay someone to have her apartment vacated and cleaned out. But she was not going to set foot inside it or the hospital again.

She was going home. As soon as she could arrange a plane ticket. Getting into a taxi, she asked where she could get a room for a decent price.

When he named a nearby hotel, she asked him to take her there. By the time they arrived a few minutes later, her tears had dried up.

No more crying. Hadn't she learned from her childhood that tears changed nothing?

All they did was make her throat ache and her head hurt. The only way she could alter her current situation was with common sense and a firm resolve not to look back.

She took her wallet out and pulled out a few bills to hand the driver. Something fell onto the seat when she did. Picking it up, she saw the ticket to the carol service that Theo had given her a lifetime ago. She'd taken it out of the notebook a couple of days ago, thinking they might actually go together.

That was a laugh.

Handing the driver the money, she got out of the cab, still looking at the ticket. It was in two days' time. The last two weeks had been a whirlwind of activity, followed by a devastation unlike anything she had ever experienced.

Well, she had at least two days until she could get a flight to the States, especially at this time of year. She might as well do some sightseeing while she was here. It might help ease the pain in her heart or at the very least it would fill her time and keep her from thinking about all she'd lost.

Lost?

She'd lost nothing except a thin layer of pride and maybe a little of her self-respect.

Those would come back soon enough. At least she hoped they would. Until then, she would take in some sights and maybe listen to a few carols.

You didn't have to like Christmas to like music, right?

She walked up to the hotel and asked for a room for a few days.

"How many days?" the man at the front desk asked.

Swallowing, she gave the only answer she could think of. "As many as it takes."

He didn't ask her to pin down her dates, and she was actually shocked that they had a room. But maybe there'd been a last-minute cancellation. Why couldn't she have gone somewhere like London for her working furlough?

Because she'd been called in for Ivy.

The man at the desk handed her a key and pointed to the elevator. Here she went again. It seemed like she was forever going up and down in the things.

Kind of like her life.

One minute she was soaring high, and the next she was sliding back to earth with a bump.

Well, she was about to get off this particular carnival ride once and for all. And as soon as she got on that plane, she was going to put her time in Cambridge behind her and never look back.

And that included a certain little girl and her devastatingly handsome and equally dangerous dad.

He'd hurt her. He'd known it the second she'd backed out of Ivy's room two days ago. When he'd been able to finally untangle himself from the sheets on Ivy's bed and rip open the door, he'd come face to face with Naomi, rather than Maddy.

"Where is she?"

Naomi didn't ask who he meant, she just pointed down the corridor.

By the time he got to the elevator, though, she was gone.

He'd acted like an ass ever since the night at the hotel. He'd done his best to avoid her, rather than sitting down and talking about what had happened like an adult.

And this was the result of it. He'd come in to find a resignation note sitting on his desk, delivered by a special courier service. The formal letter had no address on it, and when he'd checked at her apartment later that day, the manager said she'd already vacated the place. In two days' time? How was that even possible?

Maddy was a pretty determined woman. If she wanted something done, she would move heaven and earth to make sure it happened. Just look at Ivy's miraculous recovery. Without the diagnostician's stubborn resolve to find the cause of her condition, who knew if Ivy would be getting one good report after another, like she was now.

Hell, he'd screwed things up so badly. And now there was no way to make it right.

Checking on Ivy and fielding questions about Maddy's whereabouts as best he could, he then headed over to her office. It hadn't been cleared out, but then again there wasn't much here that gave evidence that she'd once occupied this room. He touched a couple of file folders, smiling as he came across Ivy's. All done now. As if she'd been an angel who'd come to help his daughter and had flitted away once her task was complete.

Who knew. Maybe she *had* been sent there by some heavenly realm. Ridiculous. She was a woman. Flesh and blood. He'd seen that first hand.

He went around the desk and opened one

of the top drawers, frowning as a familiar notebook came into view. She'd left that here?

Why wouldn't she? She didn't need it anymore, her resignation told him that much.

He flipped the book open to the first page and stopped. His eyes slid over words that made no sense. What did this have to do with patients?

This looked more like a… Like a Christmas list.

*We were just making some plans for Christmas.*

Wasn't that what she'd said when he'd found her sitting on Ivy's bed with this very notebook?

Which would mean this list was Ivy's.

He re-read the words. His heart lurched to a stop and then took off way too fast, galloping in a way that left him short of breath. This was what Ivy wanted for Christmas?

He sat down in the chair behind Maddy's desk.

No. It was no longer hers. She'd left without a word. Not to him. Not to Ivy.

The list was heartbreakingly simple, with each entry followed by a short explanation as to why Ivy wanted it.

*Make Daddy love Christmas. Because he is too sad about Mummy.*

*A new stethoscope—in purple, if Santa has one, because that's Ivy's favorite color.*

*A book about horses so he'll fall in love with them like she has.*

*An adult coloring book. One of Ivy's nurses talked about how every grownup should have one.*

*Macaroni and cheese. Evidently Theo's favorite food. Santa must carry casseroles around in his toy sack.*

*A puppy. Ha! Wouldn't Theo love coming home to find a puppy under the tree?*

When had Maddy planned on showing him this list? Or had she just written it to placate Ivy? No, he couldn't see her doing that. What he could see her doing was tracking down each of those items and sitting on Ivy's bed while they wrapped them. Except maybe the puppy. And that devastating first item. He'd done his best to make Christmas special for Ivy and she'd seen right through his efforts. Damn.

Well, he'd made a mistake in not talking to Maddy about what was happening between them. He wasn't going to make a second mistake by tossing this book back in that drawer and acting like he'd never seen it. It was time he started living life honestly. Starting with his daughter.

He went down to her room and found Judy inside. The housekeeper glanced up. Maybe she saw something in his face because she got up from the chair and came over to him, touching his arm. "I'll give you two some time together. I need to go home anyway and do laundry."

Since Judy had only brought his laundry to him yesterday, he doubted that was the truth, but he appreciated her tactful way of sliding out of the room.

Once they were alone, Theo went to the side of Ivy's bed and sat on it before lying down with his head next to hers on the pillow. He got straight to the point. "I found this in Madison's office."

He held up the little book.

"She likes to take notes in that."

"Yes, she does." He flipped through the pages. "She also writes other things down. Like Christmas lists."

"Mine?"

"Yes."

"Then you know what I asked Santa for Christmas." A note of wistfulness crept into her voice.

"I do."

She blinked and looked up at him. "Does it have all of them in there?"

"How many did you have?"

"Not many."

"That's funny. I couldn't tell if this was a list of things for me or a list of things for you."

"It's both, Daddy. I put things I thought we would both like."

Okay, well, the puppy was definitely all hers. And probably the book about horses too. But those other things…

He screwed up his courage before asking the big question. "What makes you think I don't like Christmas, baby?"

She shrugged. "It's when Mummy died. You get sad every year, even though you smile and act all happy and stuff."

"You could tell, huh?"

"Yes." She held his hand, her tiny fingers gripping his tight. "And I was thinking about that. If Mummy's in heaven, does that mean I can never have another one?"

"Another what?"

"Mummy. Because I know someone I would like."

His lungs tightened, threatening to suffocate him. "I know. I heard. But I don't think that would be a very good idea."

"Why? Mummy would like her. And I think you like her too."

He did more than that. He loved her.

Hell, why hadn't he seen that sooner?

Because he'd been too blind to see what had been staring him in the face.

"I do like her, but there's more to it than that. No one can ever take your mummy's place."

"I think Santa has magic. He can make it happen."

"Did you tell Madison any of this?"

"No."

She probably didn't even remember telling Maddy she wished she were her mother.

"Santa can't always grant every wish."

"I wished he would make me better for Christmas and he did. I can almost pedal the bike in the playground."

She'd taken to referring to the physical therapy room as the playground because it was more fun than work.

"Yes, he did. And I am very grateful for

that." That hadn't been the work of Santa but the work of the woman he'd driven from his life with his guilt and his own foolish insecurities.

"Well, I think he can make Madison want to be my mummy too. Do you want her to be?"

"It doesn't matter what I want."

"Yes, it does." Ivy's voice went up, her chest rising and falling in agitation. "You have to want it too, or the magic can't happen."

He leaned over her and put a hand on her shoulder, shocked to find she was trembling. "I don't know where Maddy is, Ivy."

"Just ask Santa. He knows. He can show you. I think she makes you happy and can make you like Christmas again."

An icy hand closed over his throat as he realized his daughter spoke the truth. Maddy did make him happy. Happier than he'd been in a long time.

"How about if I try?"

"Do you promise to try really hard, Daddy?"

"Yes, Ivy. I promise."

He'd wandered the city, going from one hotel to another. There had been no one with the name of Madison Archer at any of those he'd checked. He was almost out of time. And almost out of hope. It was Christmas Eve and in trying to track down Maddy he hadn't had time to buy any of the other gifts on that list. Because he had a feeling that there was only one present that really mattered to his daughter.

*I'll tell you when to worry.*

"I don't mind telling you, I'm worried. Worried I won't find her. Worried my daughter will have her hopes crushed. Worried that even if I do find her, she'll laugh in my face."

Theo had no idea if he was talking to God or to the jolly old gift-giver himself, but maybe it was both.

He looked up and spotted King's College. The carol service was today. He glanced at his watch. It was close to the time, actually. He hadn't had any luck in finding her and he was out of ideas at the moment, so he may as well go in and rest for a while and enjoy the service. Maybe something would come to him during it. If the worst came to the worst he could ring her hospital in the States and see if they had a revised return date for her.

Making his way to the door, he showed his ticket and went in. There was still half an hour before the service started so he glanced around the pews, looking for a likely spot. His eyes passed over a woman who had hair that looked remarkably like...

He took a step closer. It was the same length, the same sexy waves cascading down her back. And the way the light caught those highlights...

He walked up to the pew and looked past a few other people who were seated there as well. Shock pulsed through him. It was Maddy. She was staring down at the order of service, then reached up to quickly brush something from her left eye.

Tears?

His heart threatened to break in two. He made his way down the pew, apologizing for having to squeeze past the others who were already seated there.

He reached her and sat next to her.

She glanced over and her eyes widened. "Theo?"

"Mind if I join you?"

"Well... Um... I guess not."

The chapel grew silent as the service was about to begin, and he hadn't had a chance to say any of the things he wanted to say. But he'd found her. Somehow. It was a first step.

He just hoped she would listen to what he had to say when the service ended.

"Can I talk to you after this?"

"About what?"

He produced the notebook from his pocket. "I may need help with one or two of the items on this list."

Her eyes met his. "I was going to give that to you, and then we kind of got caught up in…"

"Yes. We did." He reached and took her hand, relieved when she didn't immediately jerk away from him. "Will you hear me out afterwards?"

"Do I have a choice?"

"We always have a choice. But I hope you'll let me explain a few things."

A plaintive voice in the group of robed choristers sang the opening words of the first carol. And, like the magic that Ivy had talked about, Maddy's fingers tightened around his.

He wanted to sit here with her forever, but all too soon the service ended and people began to rise from their seats to leave. He'd been here year after year, but he couldn't remember when he'd enjoyed it more. Maybe it was because of the woman seated next to him. She'd healed Ivy and if all went well, she might very well heal his heart. If not… well, that particular organ would never be the same.

"Can we walk?"

"Okay."

They left the chapel and walked back to the front of King's College, facing Market Square. Theo found them a small bench a short distance away.

He turned toward her. "First I want to say I'm sorry for how I acted after that night at the hotel."

"Okay."

It was the second time she'd used that word to answer. Maybe he'd better up his game.

"I haven't felt like that with a woman in… well, ever."

Her head tilted. "Not even Hope?"

He thought back over the years. Yes, he and Hope had shared some wonderful memories, but it wasn't the same. What he'd felt for her was packed away in a box and had been for a long time. "What I feel for you is different from what Hope and I shared."

"What you feel?"

"I love you, Maddy. I'm not sure when it happened, but it did."

Instead of looking relieved, she frowned.

"Is this because of what Ivy said the other day at the hospital?"

It took him a moment to figure out what she was talking about.

"You think I'm telling you this because Ivy said she wanted you to be her mother?"

"Are you?"

"No. I would give my daughter the world if I could, but I would never ask someone to marry me just to give her a mum."

Her mouth opened and then closed. "Did you say…?"

"Yes. I said ask someone to marry me." He took both of her hands in his. "What I said is true, Maddy. I love you. And if you feel even a smidgen of love for me, I want to walk down that aisle with you the same way that Alice and Marco did this past Saturday."

Before she could say anything, he went on. "The one thing that can guarantee that I'll like Christmas again, that is if I can spend the rest of them with you and Ivy. And then you, when she's all grown up. Thank you for saving her. And thank you for saving me. For making me realize I've been wearing a funeral shroud that wasn't mine to wear. I belong here…among the living. And I want to spend the rest of that living…with you."

She didn't say anything for a long moment. Was he too late?

He cupped her chin. "Maddy?"

"I'm afraid to believe any of this is real. It's like magic. I was sitting in that chapel thinking about you, and suddenly you were there."

"It is magic. Ivy told me I had to want it or the magic wouldn't happen."

"What magic?"

"The magic of love." His hand slid up to touch her face. "I do want it, Maddy. I hope you do as well."

Her eyes closed, and for a horrible second he thought she was going to turn him down. To get up and walk away and leave him sitting there alone on the bench.

Then they reopened and what he saw shining from the green depths gave him hope like he'd never had before. "Yes, I do want it. I love you too. That night after the hotel, I thought you were feeling guilty, like you'd cheated on Hope. And I already knew that I loved you. It just about killed me. And the way you looked at me in Ivy's room when she said she wished I was her…"

"I was embarrassed that she'd put you in that kind of a spot. I tried to get up to follow you, but I got tangled up in the bed and almost fell out of it, trying to get free. By the time I reached the corridor you were gone. And when I checked at your apartment the next day, you'd already moved out." He leaned down and kissed her. "I was so afraid I'd never find you again."

"I think that's why I haven't bought my ticket back to the States yet. I was going to call yesterday. And then today. Only I didn't. I finally decided as I was sitting in the chapel that I was going to go back to the hospital and have it out with you before buying it."

"Then let's have it out. Will you marry me?" He toyed with her ring finger before lifting her hand and kissing that spot.

"Yes, Theo. I will."

Their lips met, softly, gently and then with growing passion. By the time they pulled back, Theo's blood was pounding in his ears. "I think we'd better go back before I do something that will get us both arrested."

"Go back?"

"To the hospital to see Ivy, first of all. And then maybe back to my office. Have I ever told you that my couch there is very comfortable?"

"I've slept on that couch so I think we're in agreement as to its comfort."

He smiled and rose from the bench, tugging her up with him. "I mean it's *very* comfortable. It's also large enough for two people."

"Theo! Are you suggesting we do something indecent on that couch?"

"I'm suggesting it's the closest place that I know of."

"Definitely closer than my hotel room."

When she told him the name of it, he laughed. "That is one of the few places I didn't check."

"You looked for me?"

"Yes. I spent a good part of today checking hotel rooms and airline flights. It was like you'd vanished into thin air. I half suspected you were an angel sent to rescue Ivy and me."

"Angels don't do indecent things on office couches."

"They don't?"

"No. But then again I am no angel. I'm a woman in love."

She leaned her head against his shoulder. "Oh, Theo, look at the lights."

The Christmas lights were glowing with hope and the promise of a new year and a new start. Out of nowhere, light snow began to fall, soft flakes drifting into her hair. "They're beautiful."

"What was it Ivy said to you?"

"She said you have to believe, or the magic won't happen."

She reached up to kiss him and then regarded the snow, which was beginning to come down harder.

"I believe, Theo. So let the magic begin."

# EPILOGUE

THEO HAD HIS purple stethoscope and Hope
had her new picture frame. It seemed that
Maddy had secretly purchased the frame the
day they'd shopped for wedding apparel for
Marco and Alice's ceremony. Most of the
other items from his daughter's wish list had
been bought in a mad dash after the carol
service yesterday afternoon. Those had been
opened in Ivy's hospital room early this morning. All except for two special items, one of
which was waiting at home with Judy and
the other was hidden in a very special place.

Nestled close to him, as the hospital
pulled out all the stops for Christmas Day,
was Maddy. He could barely believe she'd
agreed to stay in England and work through
things with him. He was the luckiest guy on
the planet. At least he hoped he would be,
very soon.

He squeezed her hand as Father Christmas made his way to the center of a circle of young patients and opened his red sack. Reaching in, he fished out the first of the presents. Ivy was in that crowd of kids, her eyes bright with wonder.

"Ho-ho-ho!" The red-suited character set his bag on the floor with a thump. "I think we have something here for Grant Williamson." He handed the wrapped parcel to Evie, whose fingers lingered over his for a second longer than necessary.

"Wait," Maddy whispered in Theo's ear, her breath warm and silky. "Is that…?"

"Ryan? Yes, but don't tell." He pressed his cheek to hers, uncaring that some of the staff members were looking at them in open speculation.

It didn't matter. All around them were couples, new and old, who were celebrating the day: Ryan and Evie, Finn and Naomi, and across the room from them were Alice and Marco—not here in person, since they'd already arrived in Italy, but they were watching the festivities live via computer. A magic swirled in the air that had nothing to do with Christmas presents or the snow-covered landscape that glimmered just outside the window.

It was love.

Theo could barely believe he'd found Maddy at that carol service. To go from the depths of despair to a joy greater than anything he could imagine boggled his mind and made his heart sing.

Gifts continued to be passed around the room and opened with much laughter and delight. It was wonderful to see their patients—some of whom were quite ill—smile. Ryan would visit those who couldn't leave their rooms and hopefully spread a little happiness to them as well. It was amazing how love could heal.

It had healed him. And Ivy.

"Do you think you could put Hope's picture somewhere other than your office?"

"Sorry?" He glanced down at Maddy as Santa fished for another present.

"It should be where Ivy can see it and grow up knowing how much her mother loved her."

A strange pressure formed behind his eyes. Maddy hadn't known that kind of love. But if she would let him, he would spend the rest of his life showing her what it meant to be loved as an adult. "I'll find a good place for it. Thank you."

She leaned against him, and any lingering tension seemed to drain from her body.

"Ivy Hawkwood, it's your turn."

The sound of his daughter's name made him put his arm around Maddy. "Here we go."

Evie knelt in front of his daughter, who was a few feet away from them. She handed the girl a plain white envelope.

He could almost feel Ivy's confusion. Everyone else had received a festively wrapped box. Since he hadn't been sure this would actually happen, there'd been no time to wrap it. Judy had snapped a picture and sent it to his phone. Theo had barely been able to print it and get it to Ryan before his friend had gone off to dress in his costume.

Everything Maddy had promised had come to pass. She'd pinpointed Ivy's problem and had put his daughter on the fast track to a normal life.

Only because they'd made love, she'd insisted. If her legs hadn't fallen asleep, she might not have thought of the fistula. At least not right away.

He had no doubts, however, that she would have figured it out with or without that clue.

"She's going to love it," Maddy said.

"I hope so."

Ivy ripped open the envelope and the photo fluttered to the floor. Picking it up, she stared at it for a second or two. Then she whirled around to face them. "Is this…? Is this…?"

When Theo nodded, her eyes widened and she snatched the picture to her chest. "He looks just like Doodle!"

The therapy dog had made a huge impression on Ivy. He remembered wondering how smart it was to let her get attached to him. But he'd come to realize that sometimes you just had to take a chance and trust fate.

"*She* is the same color, but she's a toy poodle so she won't get quite as big as Doodle." He reached down and tweaked the photo. "But with her curly coat, I thought she'd be a good reminder. She's at home with Judy."

"Oh, Daddy, thank you so much! I can't wait to see her!" She leaped up and hugged them both.

"You're welcome, sweetheart."

"That's brilliant," said Evie as she stood. She paused then raised her brows in question. "But I know something even more brilliant. May I?"

Theo nodded. "I think this is the perfect

time." The perfect time to trust fate—at least he hoped it was.

Ryan reached an arm deep into his bag, soon finding what he was looking for.

"I have one item left."

Maddy glanced at the group and Theo knew exactly what she was thinking. Everyone had already received a gift.

"Madison Archer."

Evie carried the tiny present over to them, but instead of handing it directly to Maddy she handed it to him. "I'll let you do the honors."

Maybe he should have waited to do this in private, where he wouldn't be publicly crushed if she turned him down.

She wouldn't, would she? She'd told him she loved him. He needed to trust that she'd been telling the truth.

Turning the present over in his hands, he found the taped tab and quickly unwrapped it, revealing a small velvet box.

"Oh, Theo…"

There was no room to kneel with the crowd around them, so he settled for snapping the box open to reveal a diamond ring. He had done some scrambling of his own last night and had called in a favor from a friend—the owner of a local jewelry store who'd reopened his shop just for him.

"I want to be with you. Not just today. Not just tomorrow. But always. Will you marry me?"

She wrapped her arms around his neck and buried her face in his chest. For a long tense minute the room was quiet. Then a muffled "Yes" rose to his ears.

"*Stupendo!*" Marco's exclamation was the first to break the silence, his fist raised in triumph. "Congratulations, you two."

Finn came over, echoing Marco's sentiment. "It couldn't have happened to a better couple," he said, while Naomi caught Maddy up in a tight hug. More and more people filed over to offer their congratulations, the sincerity of their smiles obliterating any hint of awkwardness.

By the time things died down enough for him to actually put the ring on his soon-to-be bride's finger, people were moving to the other side of the room, where tables of refreshments had been laid out. Soon it was only him, Maddy and Ivy in their little corner.

His daughter handed him the notebook that had started it all. "What about my last wish?"

Theo smiled, taking the book from her and opening it to the first page. By now he had it memorized. "Which one? I think they've all been answered."

"There's still one left."

It seemed like an eternity since he'd watched Maddy pocket that notebook and wondered what secrets it contained. Now he knew.

He took a pen from his pocket and checked off the bullet point next to *Puppy*. "How about that?"

"No, not that one." She grinned, but there was a slight quaver of uncertainty in her voice.

"I know which one you mean. And, yes, it's been answered too."

With that, he checked off *Make Daddy love Christmas*. While he was at it, he circled the key word in that phrase, kissing his daughter's head and sending her off after something to eat.

"Finally. I thought I would never get you to myself." He set the notebook down.

"Do you?" Maddy whispered, her fingers going to his face. "Do you really love it?"

"I do. Almost as much as I love you. Now and forever."

"Me too." She tugged him down for another kiss as the lights on the nearby tree winked their approval. "Oh, yes, Theo. Me too."

\* \* \* \* \*

*Welcome to the*
*Hope Children's Hospital quartet!*

**Their Newborn Baby Gift**
*by Alison Roberts*
**One Night, One Unexpected Miracle**
*by Caroline Anderson*
**The Army Doc's Christmas Angel**
*by Annie O'Neil*
**The Billionaire's Christmas Wish**
*by Tina Beckett*

*All available now!*